PIPE DREAM

"Tell me your *real* purpose for coming to Reno."

"I already have."

"You're a poor liar, Mr. Long. I think you're a federal officer sent from Denver."

"You've got me all wrong," Longarm said, deciding that he would probably be shot if he confessed his true identity.

"I'm sorry you said that," the man told him in a tone that sounded genuinely full of regret. "Because you have left me with no choice but to kill you where you stand."

Longarm was not about to stand still and die, so he tensed and was just about to throw himself at his abductor when a voice from the bushes cried, "Drop that gun!"

The pipe smoker whirled for an instant to see who was crashing through the brush, and when he did, Longarm sprang. The derringer exploded between them and Longarm felt a searing pain across his ribs. They grappled and then Longarm managed to slam the smoking pipe straight down the gunman's throat.

"Agggh!" the man screamed as water poured into his open mouth and Longarm smashed him right between the eyes.

TABOR EVANS

LONGARM

AND THE COMSTOCK LODE KILLERS

JOVE BOOKS, NEW YORK

THE BERKLEY PUBLISHING GROUP
Published by the Penguin Group
Penguin Group (USA) Inc.
375 Hudson Street, New York, New York 10014, USA

Penguin Group (Canada), 10 Alcorn Avenue, Toronto, Ontario M4V 3B2, Canada
(a division of Pearson Penguin Canada Inc.)
Penguin Books Ltd., 80 Strand, London WC2R 0RL, England
Penguin Group Ireland, 25 St. Stephen's Green, Dublin 2, Ireland (a division of Penguin Books Ltd.)
Penguin Group (Australia), 250 Camberwell Road, Camberwell, Victoria 3124, Australia
(a division of Pearson Australia Group Pty. Ltd.)
Penguin Books India Pvt. Ltd., 11 Community Centre, Panchsheel Park, New Delhi—110 017, India
Penguin Group (NZ), Cnr. Airborne and Rosedale Roads, Albany, Auckland 1310, New Zealand
(a division of Pearson New Zealand Ltd.)
Penguin Books (South Africa) (Pty.) Ltd., 24 Sturdee Avenue, Rosebank, Johannesburg 2196, South
Africa

Penguin Books Ltd., Registered Offices: 80 Strand, London WC2R 0RL, England

This is a work of fiction. Names, characters, places, and incidents either are the product of the author's
imagination or are used fictitiously, and any resemblance to actual persons, living or dead, business establishments, events, or locales is entirely coincidental.

LONGARM AND THE COMSTOCK LODE KILLERS

A Jove Book / published by arrangement with the author

PRINTING HISTORY
Jove edition / January 2005

Copyright © 2005 by The Berkley Publishing Group

ISBN: 0-515-13877-0

JOVE®
Jove Books are published by The Berkley Publishing Group,
a division of Penguin Group (USA) Inc.
375 Hudson Street, New York, New York 10014.
JOVE is a registered trademark of Penguin Group (USA) Inc.
The "J" design is a trademark belonging to Penguin Group (USA) Inc.

PRINTED IN THE UNITED STATES OF AMERICA

10 9 8 7 6 5 4 3 2 1

Chapter 1

It was a cool and breezy autumn afternoon in Denver when Deputy U.S. Marshal Custis Long was urgently called into his boss's office. Longarm had been playing solitaire and wondering when he would be sent out on a new assignment because sitting around in a federal building was not his idea of a good time.

"What's going on?" Longarm asked when he entered U.S. Marshal Billy Vail's office and saw the concern etched in the man's round, cherubic face.

"I'm afraid we have a big problem in northern Nevada," Billy said, pacing back and forth. "The kind of a problem that I've always dreaded but realized was inevitable."

Longarm was a big, lean man, standing well over six feet with broad shoulders and a handlebar mustache. Unlike Billy, he rarely got excited and now he raised one of his hands and said, "Billy, simmer down or you're likely to bust a gasket. You know full well that the doctor said you were not supposed to get upset on account of your heart."

"I know. I know." Billy fretted. "But this is *really* bad."

Longarm drew a cigar from his coat pocket and stuck it in his mouth. He chewed the tip for a moment in reflection, then sat down and motioned for Billy to do the same.

"Now, Billy," he said calmly, "why don't you take a deep breath and start from the beginning. "'Cause unless I am badly mistaken, the world hasn't come to an end yet, and the sun will still shine tomorrow."

Billy managed a smile and quit pacing. He sat down behind an impressive desk and leaned back in his chair as he inhaled deeply. "All right," he said, lifting a telegram. "I just got word that three federal officers have crossed the line and gone bad in Nevada."

Longarm removed the cigar from his mouth and scowled. "That *is* bad," he drawled. "And how in tarnation did so many of them go bad?"

"It's complicated."

"I'm willing to listen until I understand," Longarm assured the shorter, balding man he worked for and called his friend. "Just start from the beginning and don't leave out any details."

"Okay, Custis. I didn't know this but the San Francisco office had been hearing rumors for months that there was a lot of money being embezzled up in Virginia City on the Comstock Lode. What was happening was that the booming stock market on the Comstock was selling mining shares and the demand was so great that they were trading by the linear foot."

"I thought that the Comstock Lode mines had almost petered out."

"They've had a sudden resurgence. New and better mining equipment has made some of the old mines profitable again and there are a lot of people that are willing to jump into anything if they think they can make a quick and spectacular profit."

"So," Longarm said, "people that ought to know better are again buying shares."

"Exactly," Billy said. "I wouldn't doubt that some shysters are salting the Comstock Lode mines with gold and silver. There is no fool like a fool with gold fever."

2

"Amen," Longarm said. "But how does that tie in with the three bad federal officers?"

Billy said, "The San Francisco office had heard that the shares being sold were fraudulent and that people who were buying those shares were disappearing."

"You mean they'd turn up missing?"

"That's right. But only the bigger buyers. And then, their shares were being resold."

"Slick deal," Longarm said.

"Deadly deal," Billy corrected. "At any rate, the feds in San Francisco sent one of their most experienced deputy marshals to Virginia City and Reno to try and figure out who was behind these bogus mining shares and the missing persons foolish enough to purchase them."

"And?"

"The officer sent a telegram back saying that the graft was much worse than he'd expected and that he'd need some help. So, the feds sent two more officers over to Reno and then on to the Comstock Lode."

"This," Longarm said, "is sounding fishier by the minute."

"Indeed it does," Billy agreed. "After that, telegraphed reports came in very sporadically to San Francisco from Nevada. And, after a few months, they stopped coming in altogether."

"Go on," Longarm said, beginning to get interested.

"That's pretty much it," Billy said. "When two more officers were sent to investigate, they discovered the first three had vanished with more than a quarter million dollars in cash."

Longarm whistled softly. "That's a whole lot of money! How'd they do it?"

"Oh," Billy said, "the trio wasn't sophisticated. They learned that the Virginia and Truckee Railroad was transporting the cash down to Carson City and they simply flashed their badges, got the train engineer to shut down his locomotive and then they robbed the train's vault and took all the cash."

"Tempted by too much money, federal law officers became train robbers."

"And that's not all," Billy said. "To make matters even worse, there was a local marshal on the train, and they gunned him down in cold blood. When a passenger tried to interfere, they also shot him dead."

Longarm sighed and chewed faster on his cigar. "If there is anything I hate it's lawmen gone bad. Gives all the rest of us a black eye."

"These three were the best men that they had in the San Francisco office. They were all experienced men who had received many commendations for bravery."

Longarm came out of his seat and went to Billy's window to look down on Colfax Avenue, which was always crowded with people and wagons. The American and state flags were whipping in the wind, and he reckoned a storm was brewing.

"Billy, I haven't been to California but these three rotten apples might have worked in other places during their federal careers and I might have run across them. What are their names?"

"Ike Castillo. Jeb Ware. Cletus Bigham."

"Never heard of any of 'em," Longarm said. "And, unless I miss my guess, they probably took all that cash and lit out for Old Mexico."

"That's possible," Billy said. "No one knows. They just vanished and haven't been seen or heard from since. But the San Francisco office had another interesting piece of information."

"What would that be?"

"Well," Billy said, "not two days after the V and T Railroad was robbed, a body was found that matched the description of Marshal Ike Castillo."

"Couldn't they make a positive identification?"

4

"No," Billy said. "The man's face had been obliterated by a shotgun blast fired from close range. There was no identification on the body and it had been stripped naked and left to the buzzards and varmints."

Longarm was puzzled. "So why do our counterparts in San Francisco think it was Castillo's body?"

"Castillo only had one ear; the other had been bitten off in a fight. The corpse seemed to only have one ear, too."

"That's it?" Longarm asked.

"That's it."

Longarm decided to light his cigar. He took a few puffs and said, "Billy, there's a lot of men in those frontier towns missing ears."

"Yeah, I know that," Billy said. "But it was the left ear, same as Castillo's. And the body was the same size. Castillo had a wife but the man's body was in such bad shape that she refused to look at it. Anyway, that's why there is still a big question mark."

"Where was the body found?"

"About fifteen miles north of an old mining town called Bodie."

"I've been to Bodie. It's right across the Nevada border and sits in a desolate California valley just east of the Sierras."

"I've also been to Bodie. I went there when I was a younger man," Billy said. "And I never had the itch to go back for a second visit."

"It's a rough place," Longarm agreed. "Like the Comstock Lode. Just an old and decaying mining town that no one in their right mind would ever visit except in the hope of finding gold."

"Bodie is still alive and there are said to be several hundred people living there," Billy told him. "The dregs of the frontier."

Longarm turned away from the window. "Why send me,

Billy? Why doesn't the San Francisco office send its own officers to clean up their mess?"

"Because," Billy answered, "they've already lost five of their best."

"Five? I thought you said that they sent three who then robbed the train and took a quarter million in cash."

"I did say that. But I also said they sent two more men to investigate. And guess what happened to them?"

Longarm shook his head. "I'm not sure that I want to know."

"They also disappeared."

"Damn!" Longarm swore. "So there are five missing feds and nobody knows where any of them are?"

"Except for Castillo. They are pretty sure he was the dead man whose body was found near Bodie."

Longarm contemplated his cigar and then shoved it back into his mouth. He puffed rapidly for several minutes in silence, and Billy was wise enough not to say a word. Finally, Longarm said, "This sounds like the worst can of worms I've heard of in my entire career. Do you actually believe that five federal officers of the law went bad?"

"I don't believe anything except the fact that a quarter million dollars in cash can turn a lot of good men into thieves. As for how many of the five missing officers are alive ... or dead ... that's pure speculation. What I do know is that San Francisco is desperate to find answers and is understandably reluctant to send any more officers to Nevada. So they sent me a telegram begging for our help. They suggest we send three of our best deputy marshals."

"What," Longarm asked, "do *you* suggest?"

"Custis, you've never liked to work with anyone," Billy said. "You've always preferred to go it alone."

"I still prefer it that way."

"Why?"

"Because I don't like partners who can get me killed," Longarm said flatly. "And I don't want to be responsible

6

for getting anyone else killed. And finally, I never met a man that I wanted to be teamed up with for any length of time."

"We have some damned good men here," Billy reminded him. "Haller. Johnson. Carter. Wilson. They are all seasoned and trustworthy."

"I know that and I mean no disrespect to them," Longarm said. "But that doesn't change my mind about not wanting to work with any man."

"This case is extraordinary," Billy told him. "It demands an unusual approach so how about working with a *woman*?"

"What?"

"You heard me."

"Are you crazy?"

"Nope," Billy said. "But I think that it's clear that whatever is going on in Nevada is very scary. Somehow the people responsible for this skulduggery were able to peg a federal officer and exterminate him."

"I still say that Jeb Ware and Cletus Bigham have probably raced on down to Mexico. And the other three officers sent from San Francisco are all dead. My guess is that, except for Castillo—if that was his body they found—they are resting in the bottom of some deep Comstock mine. Those shafts drop hundreds of feet straight down and that's the perfect hiding place for the dead. It happens on the Comstock all the time."

"Well," Billy said, "you very well may be correct. But we still have to find out, and I have a contact in Reno. A woman who is the daughter of one of the missing federal officers. She . . ."

"I don't care if she is the resurrected Joan of Arc," Longarm snapped. "I won't work with a woman."

"You need an identity, and appearing to be a married man would deflect whoever is looking for just another federal officer arriving on the Comstock to investigate. This woman will also know things about the area that you do not. She could prove invaluable, Custis."

"I absolutely will not work with her."

"Very well," Billy said. "I'd already anticipated that response and sent the woman a telegram to that effect. Her reply was equally emphatic."

"What do you mean?" Longarm asked.

Billy reached down and retrieved a telegram that had come from Virginia City. He handed it to Longarm and it read: *Tell your officer to go straight to hell. I don't need him to help me find my father.*

"Good," Longarm grunted, tossing the telegram back to the desk.

"Her name is Carrie Lake," Billy said, "in case you cross her path."

"I won't."

"Don't be too sure. She sounds like a very determined young woman."

"When can I leave for Nevada?"

"Today, if possible," Billy said. He extracted his pocket watch and consulted it with one cocked eye. "The train leaves at eleven o'clock. That gives you exactly one hour and twelve minutes. Can you make it?"

"I can," Longarm said. "Just have someone meet me at the train depot with a round-trip ticket to Reno plus traveling funds that will last me a month. I don't mean to travel like a poor beggar so I expect the travel funds to be generous."

"I'll meet you there with the tickets and money myself," Billy promised.

"What's the matter with sending one of your desk clerks to the train depot . . . or are things a bit slow in this office?"

"Don't be a wiseass, Custis. It's just that I'd rather come and see you off myself," Billy said. "Just in case."

"In case of what?"

"You turn out to be the sixth federal officer to disappear in Nevada."

8

Longarm blinked and then gave his boss a wry smile. "Won't happen."

"And that," Billy said, "is probably what the missing officers from San Francisco said before they crossed the Sierras and disappeared on the Comstock Lode."

Chapter 2

Longarm liked train travel. He vastly preferred it to riding horses or stagecoaches. Traveling by train was relaxing and elegant. A man with a little money who could afford a sleeping car could catch up on his rest and do a lot of good reading. In the short time that Longarm had had to hurry back to his apartment and gather his traveling things, he'd also stuffed a sack full of newspapers and books.

Now as the train headed north to Cheyenne where it would link up with the Union Pacific Railroad, Longarm was reading about how President Grover Cleveland, preparing for his second term, had decided that it was undignified for the incumbent president to have to campaign for re-election.

"The man is a fat, lazy fool who doesn't deserve to be re-elected to office," Longarm muttered, turning the pages of his newspaper to a more interesting article about how an inventor named George Eastman had introduced a gadget called the "Kodak," which, from what Longarm could tell, was a square camera that incorporated *rolled* film. According to the article, Eastman's camera was the first ever to be marketed fully loaded. What you did was buy the contraption, take your pictures and then mail the whole thing to Eastman's factory, which returned your prints and the reloaded camera ready to be used all over again.

"I'd like to see how that deal works," Longarm mused. "Pretty nice, if the prints are of good quality."

Another article in the science section of the paper told of a Boston fella named Philip W. Pratt, who had recently designed an electric automobile. There was a drawing of the machine, and it appeared to Longarm to be a tricycle powered by huge and cumbersome electrical storage batteries.

"Who in the dickens would ever be seen on such a ridiculous contraption as that," Longarm muttered to himself. "Why, if I saw a grown man riding that on the streets of Denver, I'd probably laugh myself to death."

Longarm pulled out a copy of *Huckleberry Finn* by Mark Twain and began reading about misfortunes of the black slave Jim and Huck on the rolling Mississippi River. It was good reading; serious implications but with brilliant touches of humor, and he was enjoying it immensely. Longarm reflected that the only time he ever seemed to have these days to finish a good, long book was when riding on the train.

He made his train transfer in Cheyenne and then headed west across the rugged Laramie Mountains. Their highest peaks were already covered with snow and Longarm thought that indicated that this year would have a hard winter. The hour was growing late now and Longarm could see a full moon casting giant shadows across the darkened land.

"Laramie stop! Laramie stop!" the conductor called when Longarm exited his private compartment to stretch his legs.

Longarm waited for the conductor to appear and asked, "The usual one-hour stop in Laramie?"

"That's right, Marshal. We need to take on water and coal. And since you appear to be wide awake you might just want to get off this train and breathe in some fresh air. But I'll warn you that it's mighty chilly out there."

"I've got a heavy coat, and I do need a jolt of fresh air," Longarm said. "A quick walk about Laramie would do me good and help me sleep late tomorrow morning."

"Just don't be late getting back," the conductor warned. "We'll blow the whistle five minutes before departure for Rock Springs."

"I know. It's not like I haven't ridden with you on this run quite a few times."

The conductor, an old man who smoked a corncob pipe chuckled. "That's for sure, Marshal. I'll bet you've ridden this run at least a dozen times since I've been conductor."

"More than that," Longarm said as he grabbed his coat and headed for the loading platform where a step was being lowered.

He disembarked and the cold, biting air slapped him full in the face. The wind was blowing off the Laramie Mountains and it cut through Longarm's wool coat like a scythe through wet wheat. He buttoned the coat up to his collar, ducked his head into the wind and wondered why he'd even bothered to come outside into this chilling wind. But there were some good saloons nearby and Longarm thought he'd like to have a couple of rye whiskeys. The brand of whiskey sold on the train wasn't one that he favored, and he'd already learned that the train was out of his favorite cigars.

Longarm hurried up the street but a sudden hard blast of wind sent his flat-brimmed hat flying. The thing just shot up into the dark sky and spun like a kid's top then headed north. Longarm chased the hat down the street cussing. The hat spun high up over a two story brick building.

"Damn!" Longarm swore, furious at himself for losing the expensive snuff-brown Stetson. "Now that was sure stupid!"

Angry, he ducked into the White Dog Saloon, a favorite watering hole where Longarm knew they served Old Beaver, a good but inexpensive brand of rye whiskey. He also knew that they'd have his special brand of cigars. Like the rye, the cigars were modest in price but high in quality. Longarm had already decided to buy a dozen so that he'd have more than enough to get him to Reno, where he'd take a stagecoach up to Virginia City.

When he entered the saloon there were about thirty customers lined up at the long bar made of polished mahogany. Over the sound of an out-of-tune piano, Longarm shouted, "Sam, I'll take a couple shots of Old Beaver tonight to warm my bones."

"Why Marshal Long!" the bartender and owner said, grinning. "I didn't recognize you without your hat."

Longarm ran his fingers through his mussed hair. "Yeah, I just lost it in the wind. It's freezing up here, Sam. I'll bet that you are going to have some kind of winter."

"That's what everyone is saying," Sam agreed as he polished a glass and then filled it to the brim with the excellent rye. "First one is on the house, Marshal."

"Much obliged. And I'll need a dozen cigars. The good ones you carry from Cuba."

"Coming up," Sam said with a wink. "How are things in Denver?"

"About the same." Longarm twisted around to look at the crowd. "Lot of men here tonight given that it's midweek and the weather is so raw."

"Most of them are cowboys from the Cross X Ranch. It's owned by Morris Wilcox, an ex-senator from Wyoming."

"I've met the man."

"That's him down at the end of the bar," Sam said, leaning closer and lowering his voice. "Old Morris is as testy as a teased snake and he don't often come in here to drink but this is a special occasion."

"That being?"

"One of his favorite cowboys was gunned down just last week in front of this saloon by a drifter named Pete Allison. They're hanging Pete in the morning and that's why we've got a celebration tonight."

Longarm took a sip of his rye and smacked his lips with satisfaction. "Why'd this Allison fella shoot the cowboy?"

"Who knows?" Sam replied. "Most people think they got into the fight over a whore who works at the Pink Elephant and whose name is Gloria. I don't know. But those who saw the fight said that Allison drew down on the young cowboy and shot him three times in the chest before the departed could even clear his gun. I guess Pete Allison is pretty handy with a Colt. Not that it will do him much good when he goes to hell."

"He will have a lot of company, that's for sure," Longarm said. "And it sure sounds like the man deserves the gallows. They had better use a thick rope and hang him from a stout limb if it's this windy tomorrow. Otherwise, Pete Allison might twirl around over the tree limb once or twice and then sail off as high as my lost hat."

Sam laughed a good, loud belly laugh. "Why, Marshal Long, you are the funniest! I do declare. It's good to hear a man that can joke about such a thing in these bad days."

Longarm took another sip and said, "Actually, I shouldn't joke about such a hanging, but there's too many men in need of long overdue rope justice."

"Well, Pete Allison is one of them," Sam agreed. "But the reason that there are so many of Mr. Wilcox's boys here tonight is that Pete has sworn that his family isn't going to let him hang tomorrow morning. He swears that there will be a swift reckoning that will save him tomorrow."

"Most likely he's bluffing," Longarm said.

"These cowboys aren't so sure of that, Marshal."

Longarm surveyed the drinkers, and from their grim expressions and demeanor, he decided the bartender was right. "Does Pete Allison have a lot of family in these parts?"

"No one knows, but as you can plainly see, Mr. Wilcox isn't taking any chances of allowing the man to get free in a jail break."

"Unless I'm mistaken," Longarm said, "these men appear to be pretty well on their way to being drunk."

"I tried to hold them back a bit even if it is bad for business," Sam told him. "But Mr. Wilcox is paying, and he said to keep pouring whiskey as long as his money holds out. He's pretty loaded himself, but don't let on that I said so."

"I won't," Longarm said, thinking that if Pete Allison did have family and they came to break him from the jail, there would be a lot of lead flying and people were going to die. These tough cowboys were already too drunk to shoot or think straight.

Longarm tossed his whiskey down and ordered another. "And don't forget I need those cigars."

"Sure thing!"

Longarm was jostled by a cowboy on his right. He ignored that until the man gave him another elbow that knocked his glass of whiskey flying.

"Hey," Longarm protested. "Take it easy."

The cowboy, who was barely old enough to shave but whose eyes were bloodshot and angry, turned to Longarm and snarled, "Stranger, I ain't in no mood to be told anything. If you don't like standing beside me, then git out of here! Just go off and drink somewhere's else."

Longarm started to say something but then changed his mind. He did not want to have any trouble with a kid who was too drunk and filled with anger to be accountable for his actions. So, rather than creating a stir, he decided just to move down toward the end of the bar and finish his drink.

"Hey!" the drunken young cowboy said. "Look me in the eye like a man when I talk to you."

Longarm gave the cowboy an icy stare. "You're drunk and out of line here, kid. Don't push me."

The cowboy blinked owlishly, and then he frowned as his thoughts slowly coalesced. "Mister," he slurred, "are you insulting me?"

"Nope," Longarm said, "but I think you'd better go easy on that free whiskey. Maybe even go over to the corner, lie down and get some sleep. Otherwise, you'll be sorry tomorrow morning."

"Mister, when I need your damned advice, I'll ask for it!"

Longarm gave up and was just starting to turn and move down the bar a ways when the young cowboy grabbed his arm and then tried to spin him around so that he could throw a punch.

It had always been Longarm's policy not to mess with drunks unless it was absolutely necessary. Drunks were irrational and they'd do crazy, dangerous things. So you tried to placate them with words, and, if that didn't work, you drew your pistol and gave them a good crack across the top of their whiskey-soaked skulls. This sent them off to a sleep that they would not awaken from until they were in a jail cell and feeling like death warmed over.

So as the young cowboy unleashed a clumsy, looping, overhand, Longarm ducked, grabbed his Colt, which was turned butt forward on his left hip and drew it in a clean,

17

efficient manner. His Colt came up in a blurring arc and landed right on top of the cowboy's hat sending its wearer to the floor.

"Sorry about that," Longarm said to no one in particular, "but he was being disrespectful and needed to get some sleep."

The Cross X Ranch cowboys stared at their young companion, then at Longarm and back at the unconscious cowboy. Finally, a burly man who Longarm recognized as the ex-senator from Wyoming disengaged himself from the bar and swayed over to Longarm.

"Why'd you hit the boy on the head?" he asked.

Longarm tried to explain but the rancher wasn't in the habit of listening. Instead of agreeing that the cowboy deserved a pistol-whipping, Morris Wilcox turned to his men and shouted, "Are we going to stand for this foul action against another of our boys!"

"No!" they shouted in unison.

Longarm took a step back and raised his pistol to point it at Wilcox's broad chest. "Now look here," he said, "I am an officer of the law, and this cowboy of yours threw a punch at me without any provocation."

"Oh yeah!" Wilcox challenged. "Well Jimmy Bean is a good boy and I don't believe you."

"Believe whatever you want," Longarm said, getting angrier by the moment. "But it's the truth. And now, I suggest you and your cowboys lay off the whiskey and simmer down before you all get your heads cracked."

The ex-senator from Wyoming guffawed. "You gonna take us all on, Mister Lawman?"

Longarm said, "Sam, you have a double-barreled shotgun behind the bar. Hand it over to me."

Wilcox shouted, "Sam, if you give this man a shotgun I'll personally see that you hang alongside Pete Allison tomorrow morning."

Longarm still had his gun in his hand, and if things didn't turn around real quick, he was afraid he was going to have to use it on these men, starting with this self-important fool, ex–Senator Morris Wilcox.

Chapter 3

"Senator Wilcox," Longarm said, his voice loud enough for every one of the men to hear, "I think you and your boys ought to call it a night. Ride back to the ranch or get a room at one of the hotels. There's no point in getting drunk and in trouble with the law."

"What's your name?"

"Marshal Custis Long. I'm working out of the federal office in Denver."

"Then go back to Denver and don't stick your nose into what doesn't concern you. And furthermore, I don't like what you did to my cowboy."

"I did what I had to do," Longarm said. "Now are you going to pull your cowboys out of town?"

"Nope. We got rooms at the Staghorn Hotel. We wouldn't miss the festivities tomorrow morning for anything in the world."

"Just as long as you aren't taking part in them."

"Whether we do or not is none of your concern, Marshal Long. I'm guessing that you came in on the train from Cheyenne. Right?"

"That's right."

"Then I suggest you head on back to it right now."

Longarm probably should have taken the ex-senator's advice but damned if he liked to be prodded or pushed. The fact of the matter was that he hadn't had his second glass of rye whiskey or paid for his cigars.

"I'll be staying a bit longer, Senator."

The cattle rancher leaned in close to Longarm, his breath heavy with alcohol. He was unshaven and stunk as if he were a poor working hand instead of a gentleman of considerable importance.

"Listen," the man hissed, "I've had enough of your meddling and interference. This is a private party. A *necktie* party, Marshal. And you haven't been invited, so I'm telling you to get out of this saloon before I decide to turn my boys loose on you. Is that clear enough?"

"It sure as shootin' is," Longarm growled. "Sam, give me the shotgun. Now!"

"Marshal, I gotta make a living in this town. Why don't you just do as the senator says and move along. There are plenty of other saloons open and . . ."

Custis could see that he wasn't going to get any help from Sam, and that wasn't really surprising. He'd put the man in a bad squeeze and that had been a mistake.

"All right," Longarm said. "I'm going to have to make an arrest and I'll start with you, Senator."

"Over my dead body!"

Longarm could feel the cowboys tensing, and he knew that one of the drunken fools was bound to draw his gun and open fire. If that happened, there was going to be a bloodbath.

"Sorry to do this," Longarm said.

"Do what?"

"This," Longarm said, whipping up his gun and cracking the senator across the side of the head.

The big rancher went down just like the belligerent young cowboy, and before the other cowboys could react,

Longarm vaulted over the bar and grabbed the shotgun that he knew Sam kept loaded and ready for any emergency.

"Freeze!" he shouted, cocking back both barrels. "Anyone drunk or dumb enough to go for their gun is going to be splattered all over the floor!"

When one of the drunker cowboys went for his gun, Longarm slammed him in the guts with the shotgun and then he jumped back and yelled, "Hands up, every one of you!"

The cowboys were drunk but they could still tell that he wasn't bluffing and they reached for the chandeliers. One of them hissed, "My name is Monty Hatch. I'm the ranch foreman and you're making a big mistake."

"The mistake was the senator's for letting you men get all liquored up," Longarm countered. "Did you even consider that, if Pete Allison does have friends and family that are going to spring him from jail, you aren't going to be in any condition to stop them?"

"We'll be sober by morning," the foreman vowed, eyes bloodshot and rocking unsteadily on his feet.

"You'll be in misery and shaking like aspen leaves," Longarm shot back. "Now, I'm taking the senator and Jimmy Bean to jail, and I'm also closing down this saloon."

"We'll find another saloon," Monty told him. "No badge-totin' sonofabitch from Denver is going to tell us where or how much to drink."

"That does it," Longarm said. "Hatch, you're also under arrest."

"What the hell for!"

"For arguing with an officer of the law. Pick up the senator and that fool cowboy and head for the door. If anyone else tries to interfere, I'll blow you and the senator to pieces."

Monty Hatch was a big, tough-looking man who wasn't accustomed to being ordered about by anyone except his boss, Senator Wilcox. But when he gazed into Longarm's eyes, he seemed to understand that he'd better do as he'd been told.

"All right, boys. We don't want the senator killed by this crazy sonofabitch from Denver so let's play it his way for now. Help me get the senator and Jimmy to their feet and let's all go over to the jail."

"Now you're talking sense," Longarm muttered, careful to keep the shotgun trained on the angry cowboys. "Sam, I'll take those cigars before I leave."

"Sure thing, Marshal!"

Longarm stuffed the dozen cigars into his pocket and started to fumble for money but Sam objected. "They're free, Marshal Long. Just . . . just get out of here before something else happens and we all get shot to hell."

"Yeah," Longarm agreed. "I'll do that, but I won't forget you wouldn't give me the shotgun when I asked for it."

Sam looked away ashamed as Longarm herded the Cross X Ranch crew out of his saloon and down the street with their hands over their head.

When they reached the local marshal's office, Longarm rapped hard on the door and yelled, "Open up in there!"

The marshal peeked through the front window, saw the crowd of cowboys with their hands raised high and cried, "What's going on!"

"I'm Marshal Custis Long and I've got three men I want you to jail. Open up."

"Looks like you got about a dozen! My jail can't hold all those men."

Longarm was exasperated. "If you don't open this door, I'll blow it off its hinges with this shotgun!"

The door finally opened a crack, and when it did, Longarm kicked it hard, bowling the town marshal over backward. Longarm shoved Monty Hatch, Jimmy Bean and Senator Morris Wilcox through the door. He spun around toward the crowd of angry cowboys and warned, "If you fellas create any more trouble tonight, I'll arrest every damn one of you and have you tied to a tree until we can find a judge."

The Cross X cowboys didn't say a word as Longarm closed the door and then confronted the local marshal. "What's the matter with you? Weren't you even aware that the senator and his cowboys were working themselves up to break into your jail and hang your prisoner?"

The town marshal was an older man who looked as if he'd lived a hard and disappointing life. "One law officer can't hold off that many," he whined. "If they came, then I was going to hand Pete Allison over to 'em and hand over my badge because this job doesn't pay all that well."

Longarm had never seen this man before, but it was clear that Laramie had a weak marshal in charge of law and order. He frowned and saw that there was an empty cell. "Let's get Wilcox and his cowboys locked up. We can talk things over afterward."

The local marshal didn't help at all. He just stood back shaking his head and muttering over and over, "This is a big, big mistake. I want it known I had no part in jailing Senator Morris Wilcox."

The foreman was the last to enter the tiny cell. He looked over at the other cell to see Pete Allison sitting on his bunk. "Allison," he hissed, "you're going to die real hard. I told the hangman that the drop had better not break your neck because we want to enjoy watching you dance while you strangle on the end of the noose."

Pete Allison didn't say a word. The light in both jail

25

cells was poor so Longarm couldn't really see the condemned man's face, only his silhouette.

"Hatch, that's enough of that talk," Longarm warned as he locked the Cross X men in the second cell.

The local marshal was beside himself with worry. "Listen, my name is Marshal Dudley Potter and you have no business coming in here and creating even more problems than I already have to handle!"

Longarm tossed the jail keys on Potter's cluttered desk and regarded the man with scorn. "You don't strike me as being much of a lawman. If you'd been doing your job, you'd have gone over to the White Dog Saloon and dispersed that drunken crowd hours ago. Don't you know they were just working themselves up to busting in here and having a necktie party?"

"Yeah, so what?"

Longarm could see that there was no point in shaming or insulting Potter any more. The man was completely worthless.

Prisoner Allison finally climbed off his bunk and came over to grip the cell bars. "Don't waste your breath talking to old yellow-belly Potter. Hell, I'm surprised he didn't try to handcuff and take me over to the White Dog Saloon himself."

"Shut up, Pete!"

"Marshal," Pete said to Longarm, "I don't know or care who you are, but I will say this: You're all on your own now. You'll get no help from Potter or anyone else in Laramie. And when my friends come to town, there's going to be hell to pay."

"That's it," Dudley Potter cried, tearing his badge off his coat and flinging it to the floor. "I quit! I'm finished."

Longarm could scarcely believe what he was hearing. "You can't just quit," he protested. "This town is sitting on a powder keg that is fixing to explode tomorrow morning. You were hired to serve and protect the citizens of Laramie."

"To hell with them," Potter spat. "Do you see any of the citizens here willing to help *me*? No! They're all locked up in their homes and they won't come out until the trouble is finished. But I won't be here. I'm leaving on that westbound train for California."

Right then, Longarm heard the train whistle that was the signal for him to hot foot it back to the depot and climb on board. He had a hard assignment facing him on the Comstock Lode, and his boss wouldn't be happy if he was sidetracked or shot down by an angry mob in Laramie. But dammit, he couldn't just leave things here as they were and walk away in good conscience.

"Potter," Longarm said as the man grabbed his coat and hat, "you are a *coward* and an insult to my profession."

"You can call me any damn thing you want," Potter said, cracking the door and peeking outside to make sure that he wasn't going to be shot when he set foot on the sidewalk. "It doesn't matter to me a tinker's damn what you say or think. And, to tell you the truth, if you had any brains, you'd follow me to that westbound train and get out of Laramie fast!"

When the door slammed and Potter was gone, the condemned murderer, Pete Allison, began to laugh. Longarm turned to the man and shouted, "What's so funny?"

"You are, Marshal. Here I am locked up in this cell and facing a hangman, but I wouldn't trade places with you for all the gold in California."

Longarm went over to the cell and stared into Allison's eyes. "Is this all a bluff, or are people really coming to bust you out of here tonight or first thing tomorrow morning?"

Allison didn't answer. Instead, he just started laughing even harder.

"It don't matter anymore," foreman Monty Hatch said from the next cell.

"What do you mean by that?" Longarm asked.

"Either way, you're sitting smack in the middle of a war and you ain't going to leave this town standing."

"We'll see about that." Longarm went over to the rifle rack to check out the weapons. Like Dudley Potter, they were all worthless.

The train whistle blasted a second time, and it sounded louder and more strident. Hatch said, "Marshal, you're even stupider than Potter."

Longarm turned on the big foreman. "If you don't shut your trap, I'll come into that cell and feed you your teeth."

"Give it a try," Hatch challenged. "I ain't got anything to do until the fireworks start tomorrow morning."

Longarm was tempted but his good sense prevailed and instead he went over to Pete Allison. "I want you to know something."

"Yeah, what's that?"

"If your people do exist and they do try to break you out of this jail and save you from a legal hanging, I'm going to make sure you are the *first* to die."

Allison had been smiling contemptuously but now his smile melted and he spat at Longarm through the bars. "I may not walk out of here alive but neither will you, Senator Wilcox or Monty Hatch. And that is a promise."

Longarm wiped the spit off his chest and went back to Potter's desk. He needed another drink and he needed to think. Opening the desk, he found half a bottle of rotgut whiskey but decided that he had better abstain. It was going to be a long, tense night and he needed to be stone cold sober and ready for action come first light.

One last time, the locomotive's shrill whistle blasted into the cold night sky, and then Longarm heard the tightening of steel and the steamy hiss of the brakes being released. And then he heard the westbound Union Pacific chug out of Laramie, whistle still blasting.

It was by far the most lonesome sound that Longarm had heard in many years.

Chapter 4

Longarm propped his feet up on Potter's dilapidated old desk and studied the papers that littered its surface. There were several Wanted posters, and he studied them for awhile then rummaged through other correspondence, none of which held any real interest.

Over in the jail cell, Jimmy Bean and the senator had regained consciousness but they were feeling so poorly that they didn't raise any fuss. Tomorrow, though, Senator Wilcox was going to be in a furious rage.

"Hey Marshal," Allison called sometime after midnight. "I got a question to ask."

Longarm had, frankly, been dozing in his chair. Now, he roused and glared at the convicted murderer. "What do you want, Pete?"

"I wanted to know why anyone would be stupid enough to come into this town on a passing train and then butt into the hell storm that is about to happen here in Laramie. I mean, why didn't you just run off like old Potter?"

"Because Laramie deserves law and order."

"And you think you're the good Samaritan that will save the day? Bring peace and joy to this lousy, two-bit railroad town?"

"That's about the size of it. And I'll tell you something else."

"Shoot."

Longarm eased out of his chair and stretched. "I don't think there's going to be any trouble in the morning. I think you're the only one that will die because a man like you has no friends."

"Ha!" Pete Allison shouted. "You just wait and see, Marshal Samaritan. Come tomorrow morning before I walk up that gallows, there is going to be a hard reckoning. My family and friends will appear like flies at a picnic. One minute it will be as quiet and somber as a funeral, the next minute hell will be a 'poppin'! Just you wait and see."

"I intend to," Longarm said.

Allison began to sing a Civil War song that Longarm faintly remembered from his own time in the terrible war. It was a song about a young Confederate soldier about to enter his first battle knowing that his side was vastly outnumbered by bluecoats and that he was almost sure to die. The soldier was badly scared and pining for his family back home in Virginia. He was lamenting that he would never have the chance to marry his true love or to see his own children playing in a field of flowers.

The song was so sad and mournful that even the jail cell full of Cross X cowboys listened quietly to their sworn enemy about to be hanged. Longarm had to admit that the song brought a tear to the eye and that Allison had a fine baritone voice.

"I could'a sung it better if I had my guitar," the prisoner said when the song ended. "I can sing so sweet that it'll win the heart of a faithless whore. And I've done it many a time."

"Let me ask you a question," Longarm said.

"Go ahead," Allison replied.

"Why'd you so callously gun down a Cross X cowboy? Shoot him down like a dog without mercy or regret."

"Oh, I got regrets," Pete Allison assured him. "Regrets I got a'plenty! But they're all on account of I got caught. For you see, that innocent Cross X cowboy raped my sister two years ago down in San Antonio, Texas."

"That's a damn lie!" Senator Wilcox screamed, jumping to his feet.

"No, it ain't," Allison insisted. "And I tried to tell the judge that was why I hunted the cowboy down and plugged him in the gizzard. But, of course, the judge didn't want to hear any of that honest business. He's in Wilcox's hip pocket. Paid for all the way."

"You liar!" Wilcox cried, lunging toward the bars and thrusting his arms through them in a vain attempt to reach his accuser.

Before Longarm or the senator's men could pull Wilcox back, Pete Allison grabbed the older man's outstretched arms and slammed them downward on a cross bar with all his weight and strength.

Senator Wilcox's scream was probably heard all over Laramie. It came from deep down in the rancher's barrel chest and was a piercing, agonized sound that obliterated the sound that both of his forearms made when they snapped like tree branches. And even that didn't satisfy the condemned killer, who then slammed his forehead into the senator's beefy face and broke the older man's nose. Allison smashed his forehead into the man's face a second time, but by then, Senator Wilcox had fainted.

"Sonofabitch!" Monty Hatch bellowed, trying to get his own arms through the bars to reach Pete, who had retreated and was beginning to chuckle with mirth over the terrible damage he'd just handed out to the senator.

Hatch was insane. "I'll kill him with my bare hands!"

Longarm had his gun out and was at the bars. "Get back or he'll break your arms, too!"

Hatch retreated when Allison lunged to grab his arms, just missing. The Cross X Ranch cowboys went wild, cursing and slamming the bars but there was nothing they could do to help their boss or get some retribution.

"Everyone be quiet!" Longarm shouted.

Hatch looked up. "The senator needs a doctor fast."

Longarm ran back to the desk and snatched up a lamp. He hurried back to the cells and raised the lamp so he could see the unconscious rancher whose face was covered with blood. Wilcox was twitching and gasping for air, and it was obvious that he was in serious shape.

"I'll get a doctor. Everyone calm down!"

Longarm replaced the lamp on the desk and bolted out of the office. He hurried out in the street and grabbed the first person he saw. "I need a doctor! Go find a doctor for Senator Wilcox and run, dammit!"

The person's head had been tilted downward and was wearing a Stetson so Longarm hadn't at first realized he'd grabbed a young woman. "I'll find one," she promised as she bolted down the sidewalk.

Longarm returned to the pandemonium, and it took quite a while to get the cowboys settled down. "How is your boss?"

"He's dead," Monty Hatch said, lips twisting down at the corners. "The shock was too much and his heart just gave out a few seconds ago."

"Damn!" Longarm swore. He looked over at Pete Allison. "You killed him."

"Yep," the condemned man said cheerfully. "This town now owes me one helluva big favor. For that matter, so does the whole damned territory of Wyoming."

Longarm shook his head. This whole thing was becoming a nightmare.

Several minutes later, the doctor and the woman who'd gone for him burst into the office.

"Too late," Longarm said. "Senator Wilcox died of shock or heart failure."

"Oh shit," the woman swore softly. "Now we are *really* in for it."

34

The doctor went over to the cell. "Please drag the senator over here so I can check his pulse."

The still drunk and furious cowboys did as they were told. The doctor, a rumpled man whose pajamas stuck out from his pants legs found Wilcox's wrists. "Yep, he's dead all right. What a shame, but who in the devil ruined his poor face?"

"I did." Pete Allison was as calm as a skunk in the moonlight. "And I almost had the chance to do it to Monty Hatch as well."

The doctor recoiled. "I hadn't planned to watch the hanging tomorrow but I just changed my mind."

"Don't hold your breath, Doc," Allison said.

"Let's get him out of that cell and over to the mortician's place," the doctor said. "The senator would have wanted to look good at his funeral and have an open casket . . . but I don't think that would be appropriate given what was done to his face."

Longarm found the keys and unlocked the door. "Monty, you and another man haul the senator out of there, and I'll send one of you cowboys to warn the undertaker that he's got some late-night business."

"Sure thing, Marshal. But I'm telling you this right now. The senator would still be alive were it not for your blasted meddling."

"I won't argue with you," Longarm said as the foreman and one of his cowboys picked up the heavy body and carried it out into the middle of the room and laid it on the office's filthy wooden floor. "Now go warn the undertaker that he'd better get ready for some business."

Monty ducked outside and Longarm pushed the other cowboy back in the cell and locked it.

"Stranger, do you mind an awful lot if I ask you who you are and what you are doing?" the doctor said, looking bewildered and more than a little worried.

Longarm identified himself as a federal lawman and

added, "I just stopped here while the train was taking on coal and water to get a drink and a dozen of my favorite Cuban cigars. And the minute I walked into the White Dog Saloon, I knew I was in the middle of a big mess."

"You should never have gotten off that train," the doctor said. "This town is holding its collective breath just waiting for the fireworks to begin."

"I know," Longarm said. "And Marshal Potter cut and run."

"Figures," the doctor answered. "The man wasn't worth the tin in his badge. I don't know why the town council ever hired him. I told them that Potter would run at the first sign of real trouble, but they wouldn't listen."

Longarm went over to Potter's desk and sat down heavily. He'd felt rested when the train arrived here, but now he was already feeling the weight of the world on his shoulders.

The doctor knelt beside Senator Wilcox's body and closely examined the dead man's face. "Pete Allison sure made a mess of Morris. Too bad you can't hang a killer twice."

"Yeah," Longarm said, lighting one of his cigars.

The doctor came to his feet and sighed deeply. "Wilcox was my friend, but even I will admit he was a horse's ass at times. He was overbearing and very difficult, especially when drunk. And I told the man over and over again that he was living a poor lifestyle. Too much drinking and always losing his temper. And he smoked all the time. His heart just wouldn't stand that kind of abuse."

Longarm puffed on his cigar. "Well, that's all past now. Does the senator have any relatives?"

"You bet he does. And, unless I miss my guess, Monty Hatch will go tell them what happened right after leaving the mortician's office. And they'll come boiling into town about daybreak loaded for bear and wantin' to ventilate your hide and then nail it to the barn wall."

"They'll have to get in line," Longarm said. "All I know

is that I'm going to make sure that Pete Allison hangs and then I'm going to lock up this place and wait for the west-bound train. I've seen about as much of Laramie as I care to for a good long while."

"Perfectly understandable," the doctor said. "If I were in your shoes, Marshal, I'd hike on over to the livery, wake up the owner and buy a fast horse."

Longarm almost smiled. "I suppose that would be the intelligent thing to do but I just can't."

"Why on earth not?"

"Goes against my grain, Doc. I've never been a runner."

"I see." The doctor yawned. "Those cigars will kill you, you know."

"I expect to die with my boots on, Doc."

"Yes, and maybe sooner than later. Well, since there's no need here for my services, I believe I'll get out of harm's way and go home. In four or five hours, I think I'm going to get real busy."

"Good night, Doc."

When the door closed, Longarm stretched and then continued to smoke his cigar, thinking about how things could sure go sour in a hurry.

He might have dozed off for awhile, but not for more than a half hour or so. Longarm awoke with a start and then he sat up in his chair when he heard a voice shouting from outside. He drew his pistol and went to the door. Opening it just a crack, he saw that sunrise was upon the land and the light was getting stronger in the east.

"Marshal!"

Even in the half light, Longarm recognized Monty Hatch and now the man had lots of company. At least ten horsemen surrounded him, and they were all armed to the teeth.

"What do you want, Hatch?"

"We want our boys set free and we want Pete Allison right now!"

"No deal."

"Marshal, we're not bluffing."

"Neither am I."

"You are making a deadly mistake."

"Probably," Longarm answered. "But so are you, Hatch."

At just that moment, one of the riders fired. It was still dark enough to see the muzzle flash of his pistol and then Longarm felt a splinter of wood spear his shoulder an instant before he slammed and bolted the door.

"Hot damn," Pete Allison called, "the dance begins."

"Shut up!" Longarm shouted, reaching up and painfully pulling the splinter from his shoulder.

"Let us take Allison and you might still live," one of the jailed cowboys said. "Don't be a fool, Marshal. Monty is mad but he probably don't want to kill you."

"'Probably' isn't good enough," Longarm snapped, picking up the shotgun. "Not by a damned sight."

A moment later, he heard the pounding of horses' hooves and then everything was silent, but Longarm knew it was just the calm before the storm.

Chapter 5

Since the marshal's office didn't have a back door and only two small, barred windows, Longarm knew that the Cross X cowboys would have to come in the front door. And if they did, they were going to suffer the full blast of his double-barreled shotgun, which would result in a total bloodbath. Good, but foolish, men would die and Longarm knew that he'd also have no chance of surviving the onslaught.

"What time is Pete Allison supposed to swing on the gallows?" Longarm asked in desperation.

"Eight o'clock!" one of the jailed cowboys shouted.

Longarm looked at the clock on the wall. It was 5:45 A.M. "Let's move the hanging up two hours," he said making a quick decision.

"You can do that?" the Cross X cowboy asked in astonishment.

Longarm shrugged his broad shoulders. "I don't see why not."

"Hey!" Pete Allison yelled from his jail cell. "You can't do that to me. The judge set the hanging at eight o'clock, and I'll be damned if I want to have my life shortchanged."

"Better you lose two hours than I lose the rest of my

life," Longarm replied. He went over to the cell holding the cowboys. "Who's the town hangman?"

"Ain't one."

"Then who does it?"

The cowboys exchanged glances then one of them said, "Marshal Potter agreed to do it for an extra five dollars. He said he'd hanged men before and had the noose tied and ready."

Longarm nodded his head. "Where is the noose?"

Allison jumped up and ran to the cell bars. "Now wait just a damned minute here, Marshal! You ain't a hangman, and I ain't leavin' this cell one minute before my time."

"That's what you think," Longarm snapped. He marched over to Potter's closet and flung open the doors. Sure enough, there was a hangman's noose and damned if it wasn't tied and ready for the execution.

"No!" Allison screamed when he saw the noose. "You can't do this until eight o'clock! Do you understand me? The judge set my execution for eight! No sooner."

"I apologize for the two hours you'll lose," Longarm said, drawing his gun, getting the cell keys and walking across the room with the hangman's rope. "But, due to the extreme circumstances, you're just going to have to be accommodating this morning."

Pete Allison began to shake and retreated to the back of his cell, flattening himself against the stone and cement wall. "Marshal, you can't do this to me!"

"I admit that two hours of your life must seem mighty precious right now," Longarm said. "But I also have a hunch that you have a surprise party planned for eight o'clock. Is that when your friends and family are showing up? Or maybe they plan to ride in and break you out of this jail a mite earlier. Either way, they'll be too late."

Longarm unlocked Allison's cell. "Pete, we can do this the easy way or the hard way. It's up to you."

"Can't you understand me? I ain't going early!"

"I could shoot you right between the eyes, and I will at the count of five," Longarm told the now cringing prisoner. "One. Two. Three. I'm not bluffing. Four . . ."

"Okay!" the man screamed when Longarm cocked back the hammer of his pistol.

Longarm had the prisoner turn around to face the back wall. He roughly tied Allison's wrists together with the hangman's rope, and then placed the noose over his head. "Let's go, and try to act like a man when we climb that gallows."

"You fool!" Allison screamed. "Don't you know that Monty and his friends out there are going to open fire on us the minute we step through the doorway? We'll both be shot to death."

"Maybe," Longarm said, thinking the man was probably right. "But there's no other way out of this fix that I can think of."

When they reached the door, Longarm tightened the noose around Allison's throat and eased the door open. "Hatch!" he yelled. "Listen to me clear. I'm bringing Pete Allison out right now and we're going straight to the gallows. It'll be a hanging, but not a lynching. Do you and your friends understand me? If you open fire, you'll put this man down the easy way, and I'll have to charge you with murder."

Longarm waited but there was no reply.

"Murder!" Longarm shouted. "And you'll be the one who hangs."

Allison was sucking wind as if he'd run ten miles. He was shaking hard, too. Longarm prodded his spine with the barrel of his Colt and said, "The hardest part is the waiting so let's get this over with."

"We'll never reach the gallows," Allison warned him. "Hatch and his fools will open fire on us both. But at least when I die I'll know I'm taking you with me." He snorted like a young horse and blew air out his nostrils. "Okay, Marshal."

Longarm shoved the door open wide and kept his prisoner directly in front of him as a shield. He had never felt his life was in more immediate danger than it was this very moment. They crossed the sidewalk and stepped down into the dirt street. Longarm saw out of the corner of his eye that the sun was just up from the horizon, glowing like a big fireball.

"Faster," Longarm ordered in a voice that did not sound like his own.

"Bet you wouldn't walk fast either, if you were going to that gallows."

Longarm couldn't argue the point.

The gallows loomed up ahead of them. It was a crudely built structure made with scraps and pieces of discarded building lumber. Longarm looked around for Monty Hatch and his friends but didn't see a soul. Still, he knew that not only eyes, but guns were pointed at himself and at Pete Allison.

"Climb those stairs," Longarm ordered when they got to the gallows.

"No," Allison said. "I ain't going to do it, Marshal. So you can just shoot me in the back, if you want. But I won't climb them. You and the rest of this town can just go straight to hell."

"The only one going to hell this fine day is you," Longarm told the killer.

Suddenly, a rifle cracked from somewhere across the street and Longarm felt Allison's body jerk. A split second later, what seemed like a hundred guns and rifles opened fire. Longarm felt lead flying all around him but mostly impacting Pete Allison who initially lifted up on his toes, then collapsed. Longarm knew the man would be dead before he hit the ground and that his own death was just a heartbeat away. He dove for the underbelly of the gallows scaffolding with his own gun up and blazing. The scaffolding was being splintered to shreds as Longarm rolled over and over until he was back far enough to be out of sight and at least had partial protection behind a pile of discarded gallows lumber.

He saw Monty Hatch jump up and come running across the street shooting. Longarm laid his Colt across his forearm and drilled the man through the forehead. Hatch's long legs shot out from under him and he landed flat on his back, boot heels scratching the hard dirt.

"Enough!" Longarm shouted.

The Cross X men did stop shooting. But just when Longarm was thinking that everything was starting to show signs of real sanity, he heard the thundering of hooves and turned to glance up the street.

"Oh damnation!" he muttered. "They must be Pete Allison's friends come a'chargin' to the rescue. And wait until they discover that Allison is dead."

That was exactly who the horsemen were. And when they saw the Cross X men, they jumped off their horses and started what amounted to a Wyoming war. So many bullets were flying that Longarm had no idea how many men were involved, but there must have been at least thirty.

"Pete Allison is dead!" he yelled into the smoke and din, wondering if it even mattered.

Either nobody heard, or maybe they were all liquored up and itching for a fight. Whatever the reason, there was no letup in the shooting.

Longarm knew it would be suicide to try to stand up and yell for a ceasefire. And when a bullet creased his neck and his own blood started to flow, he decided the best and only thing that he could do was to get out of town while he was still in one piece.

And perhaps it was the coward's way out, but Longarm had had about all of Laramie that he could stomach. There was an eastbound train coming through this messed-up town soon, and he'd take it back to Cheyenne, and then catch the westbound in the morning. And when he returned to Laramie tomorrow on the westbound Union Pacific, he'd see if he could sort out the pieces, providing anyone fighting was still alive.

Actually, Longarm didn't much give a damn at this point. He had a big enough mess to take care of in Nevada, and that's where he was heading with no more detours.

Having made his decision, Longarm inched backward keeping his head low, and then he jumped up and sprinted to safety between two buildings.

"Maybe old Potter was smarter than I gave the man credit for," he muttered as he headed up an alley toward the train depot while, behind him, two parties of complete fools shot up themselves and downtown Laramie.

Chapter 6

Longarm did stop in Laramie the next day on his return westward, but by then everything was peaceful despite not having a town marshal. He checked in on the jail, which was empty, and there was nothing to indicate all the trouble that had taken place the day before.

"Sam," he said when he entered the White Dog Saloon, which was silent and all but empty. "I'll have some of that good rye whiskey and a dozen more of those excellent Cuban cigars."

"Say, Marshal Long," the owner said, looking ashamed. "I'm really sorry about . . ."

"Forget it," Longarm told the man. "I put you in a terrible spot. I should have remembered that you have to make a living in this crazy town."

"Yeah, but I still should have . . ."

"It's over and done," Longarm said, putting the matter to rest. "Pour the whiskey. I'm not missing the train a second time."

Sam poured.

"And don't forget those cigars."

"What happened to the dozen cigars that you bought from me last night?"

"I crushed 'em to pieces when I dove for cover under that damned gallows. Did all the Cross X men and Allison's friends kill one another?"

"Naw," the bartender said. "There were a few wounded but not one of them killed except for Monty Hatch. They're burying Senator Wilcox and Monty on Sunday. Be a big, big deal in town, you know. I ought to have a lot of customers after the funeral. Business ought to be *real* good."

"I hope that the Cross X boys and Allison's friends don't all come in here to drink. If they do, you could have another war on your hands, Sam. They could get drunk and shoot this place up and then kill you."

"That won't happen," Sam told him. "Pete Allison's friends were all from the Yellowstone country, and they wasted no time in getting out of Laramie after they'd had enough lead slung in their direction. They grabbed Pete's riddled carcass and lit out of town cussin'. Maybe instead of a buryin' they'll toss what's left of Pete's stinkin' body in one of them geysers and boil it like a plucked chicken. That's about what he deserves, to my way of thinking."

"Glad to hear that they're gone," Longarm said, downing his rye and ordering another quick one and then paying for his drinks and the cigars.

"That was one hell of a day yesterday, wasn't it, Marshal?"

"You can say that again, Sam."

Longarm tossed down his rye and slapped his hands on the bar. "Well, I think I'll head back for the train." He checked his Ingersol pocket watch. "I've got lots of time but I'm taking no chances."

"Sure, but what happened to your neck?"

Longarm had tied a bandanna around the bullet crease, but, unable to put any real pressure on the wound, it had kept bleeding for most of the night. Now, the third bandanna he'd applied was spotted with dried blood.

"Oh, it's no big thing," Longarm said. "I got nicked by a bullet in that gun fight yesterday."

"Boy," Sam said with wonder, "that's about as close as you can come to getting killed! Marshal Long, have you ever thought about changing professions? I mean, taking up a safer line of work?"

"No, have you?"

"Naw," Sam said, polishing a beer glass. "But I would if every night was like the night before last in this saloon. Yes sir, I sure as the dickens would!"

Longarm left change on the bar top and headed back to the train. He'd be glad when the whistle blasted and he could put Laramie behind him for a good while.

"Say, is that you, Custis!"

He turned around and saw a small but attractive woman standing in the doorway of the Antelope Hotel. "Yes. But you have me at a disadvantage. I've forgotten your name."

"Flora Magee," she said, winking. "And you may have forgotten me but I sure haven't forgotten you. Don't you remember the night we had two years ago? It was winter. January I think, and snowing a blizzard. The train you were taking back to Denver had to hold over for the night. I met you at the White Dog Saloon and we sure had a great night!"

"Oh yeah, I remember. We went up to a room in this hotel and you showed me that you could be a contortionist."

"I used to belong to a traveling circus. I amazed crowds with what I could do with my body."

"Yeah, I remember you amazed me with what you could do with your body."

"The body is amazing, Marshal. If you stretch and do exercises, it will be supple enough to do things that are almost unbelievable."

"You got that right," Longarm said, nodding his head enthusiastically. "For one thing, I never thought a man and

47

a woman could couple almost turned upside down. But you proved it was possible."

"Not only possible," she said with a wink. "But *extremely* pleasurable."

"Custis, have you done any of those Oriental stretching exercises that I showed you?"

"Nope. I've been afraid to throw out my back."

"Nonsense! What we did was perfectly safe and very satisfying. Wasn't it?"

Longarm could feel meat rising in his pants. "It was as good as it gets, Flora."

"So how about a repeat?"

"I've got to catch the westbound train. You see, I was supposed to catch it yesterday but I got into that mess with the Cross X bunch and Pete Allison."

"Oh sure. I've heard all about it. In fact, it's all that people have been talking about. But that is beside the point. I'm talking about you and me upstairs and upside down."

"No time for it, Flora. Maybe on my way back we could . . ."

"Who knows if either of us will even be alive by then?" she asked. "You lead a very dangerous existence, Custis. And my life is not . . . well . . . without its risks."

"Yeah," Longarm said, "I know that but I can't afford to miss the westbound two days in a row."

Flora reached up and tipped down the neckline of her dress so that Longarm could see one of her huge, luscious breasts, nipple and all. "And you can't afford to miss what *I'm* offering."

Longarm's mouth turned dry. He checked his pocket watch. "I figure I've got twenty minutes until the first train whistle blasts. Seven more minutes after that before the train pulls out. That's not much time, Flora."

"It's enough if we stop talking, climb the stairs up to my room and do what we know we do best."

Longarm was sold. "All right," he said, grabbing Flora's

hand and heading into the hotel. "But when the first train whistle blasts, I've got to go."

"Fair enough," she told him as they scrambled up the stairs.

Longarm and Flora were not shy, and they didn't waste any time in getting undressed. The harder, trickier part was getting partially upside down so that their butts were up in a corner against the wall.

"This is ridiculous," Longarm said, tipping over and sprawling on the floor with a laugh. "Just ridiculous!"

Flora grabbed his stiff manhood and kissed it like a long lost friend. Then, she said, "Doing it my way puts all the blood to the brain, which enhances the sexual sensation."

"Flora, it ain't my poor brain that needs my blood."

It was her turn to laugh, but somehow, they got into Flora's amazing position and she was skillful enough to guide his manhood into her womanhood. "All right, slow at first. Remember? If you get antsy and try to rush this, we'll bounce our butts off the wall and it won't work."

"Okay," he said, gently moving his hips to the motion of her hips. "Easy does it."

Longarm could feel the incredible sensation starting to take effect. There wasn't another woman in the world that he'd even attempt to do this acrobatic positioning and coupling with. But Flora was so amazing that he had to try again.

"Oh, good, good!" she panted, locking her legs around his upturned legs. "Now deeper. Deep as you can go and I'll hold us in that position."

"Not too long," he told her. "My feet are going numb."

"That's because all your blood is running to your head and your big sweet potato."

"I guess so."

Flora was as strong and supple as a sapling but Longarm, although very strong, was not as supple and when his arms began to shake a bit, he lost his balance, grabbed Flora and they crashed into a pile.

"Ouch!" he shouted.

"Oh my gawd, did your big sweet potato snap in half!"

"No," he said. "I lit on my shoulder. Flora, this is . . ."

Longarm thought he heard the train whistle blast.

"Flora, I have to . . ."

But she was sitting on top of him now, bouncing like a rubber ball with her head thrown back and her slim legs bent upward at the knees.

"One minute," she told him. "When I take this position and do this to you with my hot little hole no man can last more than one minute."

Longarm momentarily thought of counting off sixty seconds, but forgot when they began hollering like maniacs.

The train whistle blasted again, no doubt about it.

"I've got to run!" he shouted, tossing her onto the bed and jumping into his pants.

"We could have done it upside down if you hadn't been so damned worried and hurried over catching that silly train."

"Yeah, I suppose."

"On your way back, visit me and we'll practice. We'll take more time and do it right."

"Sure, Flora."

She jumped off the bed, nimble as a sprite and helped him pull on his boots, shirt, coat and gun belt. "And don't forget your hat."

"I won't."

"Kiss me and tell me one thing before you go, Marshal." He kissed her. "What do you want to know?"

"We crashed but it was still worthwhile, wasn't it, darling?"

"Oh, man was it ever!"

He tossed Flora five dollars even though she would never have asked for money in exchange for her unique talents and favors.

Flora kissed him full on the mouth as he was racing out

the door, down the steps and toward the now departing train.

"Wait!" Longarm shouted, running for all he was worth toward the conductor standing on the back platform who was waving frantically for him to run faster.

The train didn't wait, of course. But he overtook it with his last burst of strength. Longarm swung onto the back platform and then bent over gasping for air.

"I made it," he finally was able to gasp.

The conductor was an older, dignified gentleman. "Yes, sir, you sure did."

He sucked in the cold air and panted. "Didn't think I was going to there for a few minutes. My legs were burned-out. I was about finished."

"Well, Marshal" the conductor said, "all is well that ends well."

Longarm straightened, took a series of deep breaths and then smoothed his clothes. "Do I look presentable enough to go inside now?"

"Yes, except for one thing."

"What's that?"

"Marshal, you forgot to button your trousers and your poor wanger is wagging in the wind."

Longarm's eyes dropped and he blushed deeply before he tucked his manhood inside his pants and then buttoned up tight.

"Now you're ready," the kindly conductor said, patting him on the shoulder. "And sir, I'm delighted to see that you made the most of our brief stay in Laramie. Not many men would have been so bold."

"Thanks," Longarm said, still feeling the heat burn his cheeks as he ducked into the caboose.

Chapter 7

The conductor hurried through the train shouting. "Reno! Reno is the next stop!"

Longarm was plenty ready to get off the train. His neck wound had scabbed over and he'd done a lot of sleeping and dozing across the Great Basin where Salt Lake City lay stewing in its fetid brew of salt and alkali. He'd taken a four hour layover in Elko and visited a few friends in that old ranching town, but the last part of the journey following the Humboldt River was one of the most boring and desolate stretches of country that he'd ever had the misfortune to cross.

"You take care of yourself, Marshal Long," the conductor said as he climbed down from the train. "Gonna be staying here for awhile?"

"Might be a couple of weeks. I just don't know."

"Well, whenever you rejoin us it will be good seeing you again. And thanks for that Cuban cigar."

"You're welcome." Longarm picked up his bag and headed down Virginia Street toward the center of town. There was a fine hotel called the Maple House that he preferred and which was right next to the Truckee River. The fishing was generally good there, if the water wasn't too high or too low. This being October, he had a feeling the water level might be very low. It all depended on what kind of rains they'd gotten up in the high Sierras through the hot months of summer.

He stopped on the bridge and looked out over the Truckee and saw that the water was, indeed, very low. The river was so shallow that it could probably be forded on foot.

"Damn shame, isn't it?" an elderly gentleman said.

"What's that?"

"The water being so low. I haven't been able to catch any fish in weeks. Dry, much too dry."

"Well," Longarm said, "maybe they'll have a lot of snow this winter and the thing will be a monster come next spring."

"If so, the fishing would be just as poor as it is now," the old man said with disgust. "Too much water or too little water and you might as well forget fishing. I know. I've been fishing in the Truckee for thirty years."

"That's a lot of fishing."

"Used to be much better," the old man confided. "I could catch four-and five-pound trout from May to October. Enough to fill my creel in an hour and they had that good, firm meat you get when the water is ice cold."

"But all that has changed?"

"You bet it has! Now, the damn kids are out here with their fishing poles from sunup until sundown. They pitch rocks in the best pools, go swimming when it's hot and I'm sure they even piss in the river! Would you catch and then eat fish where a bunch of hooligans are pissing?"

Longarm stared down at a flock of mallards, several pairs of which were vigorously and loudly in the act of mating. Mating, he could see, looked to be a lot of fun for the drake but torture for the hens who appeared on the verge of getting drowned.

The old man followed Longarm's gaze. "Dirty ducks!" he snorted, wagging a finger at them like a schoolmaster might an unruly child. "I just hate 'em. Especially those vulgar, sex-crazed drakes. All they do is shit and screw. They're almost as bad as the boys who piss in the Truckee River."

Before Longarm could think of a rejoinder, the old man bent over, grabbed a rock from the road and then hurled it at the coupling ducks. He missed but startled them into a noisy, protesting flight.

"If those drakes want to behave like that, they can go elsewhere!" the old man ranted, spittle flying from his mouth. "There's still a few decent ladies and their children in Reno and they don't need to see mallards screwing like there's no tomorrow. It might put sinful ideas in their minds."

"But maybe, for the ducks, there *isn't* a tomorrow and they don't see what they are doing as filthy."

The old man was too infuriated to listen. "If it wasn't illegal, and if I weren't a retired minister and deeply respected in this community," he swore through his clenched jaws, "I'd buy a shotgun and kill every last one of those sinful drakes!"

Longarm continued on across the bridge, the retired minister still ranting and raving at the ducks that had not flown away. Some men, he knew, developed some dignity and presence in their later years. A few, however, seemed to grow even more cantankerous and violent as they aged. Longarm did not know why, but that old fella back there was dangerous and needed to start rereading the Good Book.

Normally, Longarm stayed at the Maple House, a towering brick structure right on the south end of the bridge with a good view of the river. He was well known there and enjoyed the hotel's balcony and excellent cuisine. It was a little extravagant for a federal officer but Longarm figured that he deserved to stay in a nice place when he was putting his life in jeopardy.

Now, remembering that five federal officers had already disappeared on this case, Longarm decided that he ought to stay where he was unknown and try very hard to keep his identity a secret.

"That means I need a new name and identity before I go up on the Comstock Lode," he mused aloud as he gazed up and down Virginia Street for a hotel that would suit a well-heeled mining stock investor without breaking his modest travel money account.

Reno's main thoroughfare was busy and had hotels to offer a prosperous traveler. The town itself was also picturesque and pleasant with wide, tree-lined residential streets. Because of the harsh conditions up in Gold Hill and Virginia City, many Comstock investors had chosen to build not only stately homes but also opulent business offices near the Truckee River. Reno had many stock brokerage houses and banking institutions as well as department and clothing stores where you could buy the finest chocolates, firearms and custom-made boots. Fresh flowers arrived daily on the train from California. There were at least a dozen saloons that catered to men of every social status and income level.

Longarm knew that the Union Pacific also pumped a lot of money into Reno where major roundhouse, storage and repair facilities were located. The town had prospered greatly during the heyday of the Comstock, and when the mines up there had begun to decline, Reno had hardly felt the impact thanks to its timber, ranching and many other diversified industries.

A beautiful woman passed close to Longarm and their eyes met. The woman had green eyes, black hair and a smile that could have melted the heart of Genghis Khan. She surprised him by saying, "You look lost. Can I help you find something?"

"I'm looking for a hotel. Do you have any recommendations?"

"I've heard very good things about the Maple House."

"Any other hotels?"

"Yes," she told him. "I understand the Regis is very good. A little expensive, perhaps, but of the highest quality and it's just a short way south of here. See?"

She turned and pointed. Longarm followed her gaze. "Yes, I see. Perhaps that is a little too rich for my pocketbook. I've only just arrived on the train, and I will probably be leaving for the Comstock Lode tomorrow."

"In that case," she said, "you really should pamper yourself tonight at the Regis. Have you ever been up on the Comstock?"

"Quite a few years ago."

"Well," the lovely young lady said, "it has not improved with the passage of time. In fact, it has gone downhill. The mines are not as prosperous and the hotels are in decline. Pipers Opera House is closed and shuttered as are many of the better establishments."

"How interesting," Longarm said. "I'd been told that there were new and rich mining discoveries."

"Well," she said, "I would take that information with a grain of salt and a good dose of skepticism. Anyway, good day, sir."

Longarm was sorry to see her walk on up the street. Rarely had he met a more stunning young lady. He watched her until she disappeared around a corner and then he reached into his pocket for a coin. "Heads the Regis, tails the hotel I'm standing next to."

He flipped the coin and it came up heads. With a grin, he headed down the street toward the Regis wondering if he would ever be so fortunate as to meet the stunning young woman again.

"But what should I call myself?" he asked, thinking that he would like to keep his first name to avoid confusion. So, he really only needed to change his last name.

He passed a bookstore and prominent on display in the

glass window was a sale on the works of the poet, William Wadsworth *Longfellow*.

"That's it! I will call myself Custis W. Longfellow. The name carries a good deal of panache and it certainly sounds high class."

Pleased with himself, Custis W. Longfellow went down to the Regis Hotel where he would spend the night. The long train journey and his trouble in Laramie had taken its toll. In truth, Custis was exhausted. What he needed was a good night's sleep and a few good meals under his belt. Then, first thing tomorrow morning, he would see about travel arrangements for Virginia City. He knew that the Virginia & Truckee Railroad ran daily, but it departed from Carson City, some fifty miles to the south. However, Custis was quite sure that there were daily stagecoaches that traveled between Reno and Virginia City.

"Yes, sir," the smartly dressed hotel clerk asked from behind the shining oak desk. "What can we do for you today?"

"A room, please."

"For you only?" the distinguished looking clerk asked solicitously.

"Yes."

"How many nights will we enjoy your visit?"

"Tonight only."

"Very good, sir. That will be twenty-one dollars."

Longarm swallowed hard. "I don't need the grand suite. Don't you have something a bit more . . . reasonable?"

The clerk's scowl was almost undetectable. He sized up Longarm's poor valise and his nice but rumpled and dirty clothing. "Let me check with the manager, Mister . . ."

"Longfellow. My name is Custis W. *Longfellow*."

The eyebrows shot up. "No relation to . . ."

"Of course I'm related to *Henry*. He is my favorite . . . uncle."

"Is that right. What a pity," the clerk said, looking genuinely sad.

"About what?"

"His death!"

"Oh, yeah sure. Old Henry had been ill for quite some time, however. I think it was a blessing."

"I'm sorry to hear that."

"Yes, he was a real American treasure," Longarm said. "Now, would you please see if you can find me a nice room at a more modest rate? If you do that, I will give you my autograph free of charge."

"Yes, sir! I am a great admirer of your uncle's works. My favorite of his was "The Song of Hiawatha" published in 1855, although I love "Paul Revere's Ride." Which of his many brilliant poems was your personal favorite?"

Longarm was caught. And then he remembered that the only real poem he could recite was "The Village Blacksmith." And so with a broad smile, he began, "Under the old village tree the mighty blacksmith stands . . ."

"No, no!" the clerk cried in horror. Then, in a deep and resonant voice, he raised his hands and dramatically began, "Under the spreading chestnut tree the village smithy stands, the smith a mighty man is he, with large and sinewy . . . ' "

"Of course!" Longarm exclaimed trying to look embarrassed. "How could I have possibly forgotten? Must have been that long, long ride out from my uncle's estate in New York."

The desk clerk's eyebrows shot up. "But your famous uncle was from Cambridge, Massachusetts."

"Oh yes, there too," Longarm added quickly. "Now, could you please see if you can find me a good room at a more affordable rate?"

"Yes sir, Mr. Longfellow. I'll be right back!"

Ten minutes later, Custis W. Longfellow was standing alone in one of the most impressive hotel rooms he'd ever occupied with a chilled bottle of champagne in his fist. Even more amazing, this elegant suite had been given to him gratis.

"Good choice of names, Custis Longfellow," he said, reaching for a silver corkscrew and a crystal wine goblet. "Very good, indeed!"

And that evening, as he finished his champagne, he tried to remind himself to buy a volume of Henry's poetry, the one he had seen in the nearby bookstore window.

Chapter 8

"Mr. Longfellow!"

Longarm kept walking across the beautiful hotel lobby. He had spied an abandoned newspaper, which he thought would be pleasant to read while he enjoyed a leisurely breakfast. After that, he would check out of this impressive hotel and seek transportation up to the Comstock Lode.

"Mr. Longfellow!" The hotel clerk overtook Longarm and gently caught his sleeve. "Mr. Longfellow, how was your night at our Regis Hotel?"

This was a new hotel employee so Longarm replied, "I had a restful night, and the complimentary champagne was excellent. Thank you."

"Would you be so gracious as to also give me your autograph?" He held out a paper and pen. "Because I count myself as one of your famous uncle's adoring fans."

"Sure thing," Longarm said, deciding that a good con artist could make a living at this charade. "Now," he said, handing back his fake autograph, "where is your dining room?"

"Right this way, Mr. Longfellow! And I hope you don't mind, but the local newspaper editor and the head of our Ladies Literary Society are here to do interviews on your relationship with your late and famous uncle. And, the Poets' Society would like to meet you even, if only for a few minutes. It will mean so very much to them!"

Longarm wasn't pleased. He had simply picked the name Longfellow because it resembled his own last name. And while it seemed like a stroke of genius last evening when he got a free room and bottle of champagne, now he was beginning to worry that he would become a local celebrity whose true identity would become immediately apparent because of his complete lack of knowledge about the late and famous Henry Wadsworth Longfellow.

"Excuse me," he said, coming to a standstill at the entrance to the dining room where two individuals were sitting and waving at him as if he were also a famous celebrity. "I forgot something up in my room."

The hotel clerk's look of disappointment was fleeting. "Of course. I'll tell your uncle's admirers that you will be joining them very shortly."

"Thanks," Longarm said, a moment before turning around and heading for the stairs and then up to his room.

He quickly gathered his few personal belongings then left his room, locking the door on his way out. Deciding that he could not risk going back to the lobby, Longarm found the fire exit and climbed down the rickety stairs to the deserted and littered back alley.

Longarm made his way between the Regis Hotel and another brick building until he reached bustling Virginia Street. Without looking back but nonetheless feeling a trifle guilty at his deception, he strode onto the Truckee River Bridge. It was a fine morning and the flowing water sparkled in the sun. But then Longarm saw the retired minister hurling rocks at the ducks, and he hurried on up the street in search of a stagecoach that would carry him to Virginia City.

"Excuse me, sir?"

Longarm turned to face a man almost as tall as himself.

He was well dressed and groomed, about forty years old with mutton-chop whiskers. He held a brier pipe in his left hand. "May I trouble you for a match?"

"Of course," Longarm said, finding one in his vest pocket.

The gentleman lit his pipe and got it going well before he said, "Thank you very much."

"You're welcome," Longarm told him, starting to walk away.

"My good man, is it true that you are really the nephew of Henry Wadsworth Longfellow?"

Custis stopped and turned back, realizing that this was not a chance meeting but that the fellow must have been waiting for him. Must even have had a description from one of the admiring hotel clerks. "Yes," he said, feeling even guiltier for this unplanned deception. "Now, if you don't mind, I need to catch a stage up to Virginia City."

"Certainly! But do you mind if I walk alongside of you for a moment or two? I was such an admirer of your famous uncle."

Not wishing to offend and seeing no harm in the man tagging along, Longarm nodded.

"Thank you! And what brings you to our fair city on the Truckee River?"

"Business," Longarm said, not about to elaborate.

"And that takes place up in Virginia City?"

Longarm was not accustomed to being quizzed about his personal agenda, and it did not sit well with him now. "Yes," he said brusquely and without breaking stride. "If you'll excuse me, I have some things on my mind that I need to think about, so have a nice day."

"Oh, I will," the man told him. "But *you* won't."

It was more the change of the man's tone than his remark that stopped Longarm in his tracks. "Huh?"

Longarm suddenly felt the gun jam up against his ribs as the stranger leaned closer and whispered, "You're no

63

more related to Henry Wadsworth Longfellow than I'm related to the bloody Queen of England."

"Right. Sorry about that."

"Don't stop walking, but when we reach the next corner, turn right. And, in case you haven't guessed, I've got a double-barreled derringer pressed to your side. It is inaccurate beyond twenty feet but I guarantee you that at point-blank range it will blow a hole big enough for a raven to fly through, if you should do anything other than what I order. Is that clearly understood, Mr. Longfellow?"

Longarm felt perspiration erupt under his arms and across his chest even though the morning was still cool and pleasant. "Look," he said, "you're right and you've pegged me for the fraud that I am. I freely confess that I'm not even distantly related to the poet. But that doesn't mean that I deserve to be robbed or shot."

"Turn right," the man walking close beside him hissed when they reached the corner. "And keep your hands out in front of you where I can see them. Otherwise, I'll pull *both* triggers."

"Mister, I'm sorry to disappoint but I have very little money or anything else of value on my person."

"We'll see."

The street they were walking down was not nearly as busy or attractive as Virginia Street. In fact, it was rather shabby and peopled by derelicts and hustling vendors delivering goods to the back doors of the hotels, restaurants and other businesses.

"Where are you taking me and why?" Longarm demanded.

"That's for me to know," the man said, pipe clenched between his teeth and belching a nice blend of aromatic tobacco smoke. "There is no need for anyone to get hurt or excited. Just act normal and keep walking."

Longarm didn't know what was going on. And while it was true he had used a ridiculous and false identity, which he was now beginning to regret, that was still no reason for this situation to have occurred.

"I don't suppose you want my autograph?" he asked, trying to lighten up the moment.

The man beside him chuckled but the derringer poked Longarm a bit more forcefully. "Hardly."

"Why don't I just give you my money so we can get this over with?" Longarm suggested, hoping to seize an opportunity and disarm this gentlemanly thief.

"Walk and don't talk to anymore."

Longarm cursed his luck. He'd already nearly been killed in Laramie and now this cool customer was starting to unnerve him with what would take place next. One thing was for sure, the man seemed calm and assured and acted as if he knew exactly who Longarm was and what was to be done next.

"Okay," Longarm said, deciding to take a risk. "My real name is Custis Long and I am from Denver."

"I already know that, buster."

"How?"

"I saw you get off the train and asked. It didn't cost much to gain that bit of information from one of the train's employees."

"So what . . ."

Longarm heard the hammers cock and his words were instantly forgotten. "No more talk, Mr. Long. Not one word or I'll fire."

Longarm decided that he had better do as he was being told. They continued down the street with people and places becoming fewer. Then he saw up ahead the Truckee River. There was a path along its shore and the banks below the Virginia Street Bridge appeared to be overgrown with willows and trees. That, Longarm thought, was a very bad sign.

The gunman told him to follow the well-worn footpath and they passed several fishermen who paid them no attention. One of them was reeling in a big trout and Longarm wished he could go help the man even if it meant wading into the water with a net.

"Not much farther," the gunman said.

Longarm's eyes were darting from one side of the path to the other and out onto the water. Unfortunately, just like the embittered old minister had noted, the river was low, and Longarm knew he'd have to run through thick, black mud in order to reach the main and deeper channel. But that would be slow going and it was doubtful the man who held him at gunpoint would ever allow him to reach the main current.

They entered a thick copse of cottonwoods about three hundred yards beyond the last fisherman when the pipe-smoking gunman said, "All right. This should do. Stop and turn around, Mr. Longfellow."

"I told you that wasn't my real name. My real name is Custis Long"

The gunman stepped back out of reach with his derringer in clear and ominous view. "And what is the *real* purpose of your visit to Reno and Virginia City?"

"I'd like to invest some money in mining stocks."

"Go on."

"I don't believe in investing in something that I haven't seen. That's why I rode the train out from Denver."

"Just to poke around in the Comstock Lode mines and then invest. Is that right, Mr. Long?"

"Sure, only I may not invest." Longarm tried to offer a disarming smile. "Sir, I'm no fool, and because I am not a wealthy man, I'm real careful with my investments."

The gunman appeared to be amused. "Oh, really? Well, Mr. Long, since you wear your Colt on your left hip, butt forward, why don't you reach down slowly with your left hand and extract it from your holster? Then, again slowly, toss it into the river."

"Aw come on," Longarm complained, "it's far too good a firearm to be thrown in the river. Wouldn't you rather I just toss it over toward you? It would fetch at least twenty dollars in any of the local pawn shops."

"Mr. Long, you have one second to do as I ordered."

Longarm did do as he was ordered. He tossed his six-gun but not so far that he wouldn't be able to find it in the shallows.

"All right," the man said, "tell me your *real* purpose for coming to Reno."

"I already have."

"You're a poor liar, Mr. Long. I think you're a federal officer sent from Denver to find out what happened to the ones sent from San Francisco who disappeared on the Comstock Lode."

Now Longarm understood what this was all about. This pipe-smoking man wasn't just some upscale looking mugger. Not at all. He was part of the puzzle that had brought Longarm to Nevada. The only question left in Longarm's mind was whether or not he should admit to being a federal officer.

"You've got me all wrong," he said, deciding that he would probably be shot if he confessed his true identity.

"I'm sorry that you said that," the man told him in a tone that sounded genuinely full of regret. "Because you have left me with no choice but to kill you where you stand."

Longarm was not about to stand still and die, so he tensed and was just about to throw himself at his abductor when a voice from the bushes cried, "Drop that gun!"

The pipe smoker whirled for an instant to see who was crashing through the brush, and when he did, Longarm sprang. The derringer exploded between them and Longarm felt a searing pain across his ribs. For an instant, the pain was so intense he loosened his grip on the man and they twisted around and around and then fell into the mud and shallows.

The water was shockingly cold and the mud was the consistency of quicksand. Longarm tried to wrench the derringer from the gunman, knowing it still had one more round ready to be fired. They grappled and then Longarm managed to slam the smoking pipe straight down the gunman's throat. Choking, the man hugged Longarm as they fell and rolled over and over until they were in deeper water. Longarm felt the swift current of the channel grab them both and swirl them around.

He caught a glimpse of someone running along the bank as he fought and struggled. The gunman fired but his derringer was under the current and the bullet missed. The man was trying to reach his pipe and rip it from the back of his throat but Longarm wouldn't allow it.

"Agggh!" the man screamed as water poured into his open mouth and Longarm smashed him right between the eyes.

For an instant, the choking, drowning man clung to Longarm with almost inhuman strength, trying to pull him under in a death grip. Finally his strength bled away and he sank in the roiling river.

Longarm reached down and clutched at his side, which was already going numb. His water-filled and soaked boots and clothing were pulling him under and he spotted a snagged log about a hundred yards downriver. With his strength rapidly fading he managed to reach the half submerged log and hugged it like a long lost friend.

Looking downriver, he saw the pipe smoker's head bobbing in the rapid current before it rounded a bend and disappeared.

"Custis Long!"

He twisted around and saw someone racing down the riverbank toward him. He realized it must be the same person who had momentarily distracted the gunman and saved his life.

"Here!" he shouted. "Over here on the log."

Without a moment's hesitation, the person waded into the water until it was up to her waist.

Her?

Longarm realized then that he was looking at the black-haired, green-eyed young woman he'd met the previous afternoon on Virginia Street. She was knee-deep in the water and it was spraying up into the sun like diamonds almost blinding him.

Longarm raised one feeble hand up to the sky and then he laid his head against the soggy log and tried his best not to lose consciousness.

Chapter 9

The young woman was far stronger than Longarm had thought her to be and she was also cool in a crisis. Realizing that she would be of no help out in the deeper water, the woman found a long branch from a nearby cottonwood tree and used it to reach out the last few yards to Longarm.

"Grab it!" she cried. "Grab the branch and hold on while I pull you to shore."

Longarm reached out and gripped the limb with his left hand and tried to ease himself along the submerged log. The current was surprisingly powerful at first but then it lessened its hold on him, and together, he and the green-eyed girl managed to reach the riverbank.

"You've been shot!" she exclaimed, seeing blood.

They were lying in the cold, sucking wet mud and shivering. "I don't think it's bad," Longarm said. "But I'm feeling weak."

"I can't see where you've been hit or if the bullet is still inside of you because of all the mud," she told him, absently wiping a smear across her own lovely face. "But we've got to get you out of here and to a doctor as quickly as possible. Will you be all right if I go for help?"

He looked upriver and saw two fishermen hurrying toward them. "You don't need to leave because help is already on the way."

"My name is Carrie Lake. I expected to meet you at the train depot, not in this freezing cold river."

"Sorry about that," Longarm replied.

"Sorry is no good to me. You've probably got a bullet in your belly and you're going to die."

Longarm shook his head. "Aren't you the cheerful one?"

"Well," she said, "I'm damned disappointed. I expected a highly competent federal law officer being sent from Denver that would help me find my father. Someone strong and resourceful."

Longarm was not willing to take that kind of insult and shook the woman off with his arm. "Just . . . just go cook a duck or something. These fishermen will help me to a doctor. I don't need your biting tongue."

"Can we help you!" one of the fishermen yelled, rushing up to join them. "We heard a gunshot and saw you and another fella fighting in the water. We saw the other man go under and he didn't come up for air."

"I expect he drowned," Longarm told the excited fishermen. "Can you men get me to a doctor?"

"Sure thing!" one of them said. "Al, you collect our fishing poles and tackle and I'll help this fella into town. Can you walk?"

"I can," Longarm grunted.

The fisherman ducked under Longarm to support some of his weight. "Easy does it, mister."

"I'll help," Carrie said, moving to Longarm's other side and lending her support as well. "The nearest doctor is only three blocks away. His name is Dr. Munger and the only thing I've heard about the man is that he's good at pulling rotten teeth."

"Terrific," Longarm said without enthusiasm. "Maybe

I'll have him look at my choppers after he digs the bullet out of my hide."

"Well," Dr. Munger said, stroking his scraggly goatee. "I'm afraid the bullet is still somewhere inside your body, most likely resting in your lung. I'll have to dig it out and I want to be paid my fee before I operate."

Longarm was lying on an examination table but this remark brought him bolt upright. "Pay you first?"

"Yes. In case you die, I need to have been paid for my services."

Longarm had heard enough. During his extensive law career, he had been shot, stabbed, clubbed and even speared and so had seen more than his fair share of frontier doctors. Those unfortunate experiences had led him to believe he had some expertise in judging a doctor's ability. And from what he could see of Munger's office and operating instruments, he wouldn't have trusted the man to pull a splinter from his thumb. The place was filthy with cigarette butts littering the floor and trash everywhere. Most of the trash consisted of empty whiskey bottles and wood shavings indicating that Munger spent the majority of his time drinking and whittling.

"I'm getting out of here," Longarm said, kicking his legs off the table and easing to the floor. "Where's my shirt?"

"I threw it in my trash can," Munger snapped.

"Then it's the *only* thing you've thrown in the trash. Shirt or not, I'm getting out of here."

Munger reached under his filthy smock for a flask of whiskey. "In that case, the fee for your examination is due right now. Five dollars."

Longarm was almost dizzy from the loss of blood, but he knew that if this scroungy tooth puller laid into him with a scalpel and retractors, he was as good as dead.

"Carrie," he grunted, "pay this quack and I'll repay you later. Let's get out of here."

"But you can't . . ."

Longarm's voice took on a sharp edge. "I'm getting out of this man's office even if I have to crawl."

"All right, we'll go see Dr. Eddy."

"Is he clean and competent?"

"Yes," Carrie said, paying Munger five dollars. "He's a university trained physician."

"So am I!" Munger exclaimed.

"University of Bullshit," Longarm grunted as he allowed Carrie to help him out the door.

Dr. Eddy was everything that Munger was not. His office and examining room were clean, his surgical instruments boiled and sterile, his manner entirely confident and professional.

"We need to operate right now," he said after a quick but thorough examination. "The bullet nicked one of your ribs, and I'm hoping that it was deflected and slowed down enough so that it lodged just inside the rib cage."

"In that case I'm probably going to live," Longarm said.

"Of course you are. If the bullet had penetrated your lungs you'd be coughing up bright red blood. If it had penetrated a vital organ, you'd be a corpse. I'm going to make a two-inch incision and recommend we use ether."

"No," Longarm said. "Give me something hard to bite down on so I don't wake up the dead."

Dr. Eddy looked skeptical. "Are you sure?"

"Doc, did you notice all the scars I carry? I've been through this many times before, and I don't want to be drugged."

"I see," Dr. Eddy replied, studying Longarm's bare torso. "You must be like a cat with nine lives. All right, then. We'll proceed without any form of anesthesia or pain deadeners. But, if I don't find the bullet just under that rib, then I will insist on using ether."

Longarm nodded in agreement. "Let's just get this over with," he growled.

The operation did not take more than thirty minutes, and when it was completed, Dr. Eddy held the misshapen bullet in his forceps. "There you are. Want this ugly little piece of lead as a souvenir?"

"No thanks."

Eddy looked at him. "You are a United States marshal?"

"That's right."

"Well," Dr. Eddy said, "our local marshal wants to have a word with you as soon as you are up to it. It's our understanding that you and another man were in the Truckee River and that the other man drowned while you were fighting."

"That's about the size of it."

"Marshal Parker will want to know exactly what happened and who the drowning victim was. The marshal will be along soon."

"I'd also like to know who that pipe-smoking sonofabitch who tried to kill me was," Longarm said. "As soon as your marshal shows up, send him in."

Dr. Eddy left the room and Carrie appeared. Her clothes were still streaked with mud, but it was drying and she'd cleaned it off her face. Now, she came over to stand beside Longarm. "Feeling okay?"

"Never better," he quipped. "But thanks for asking. If you hadn't had the courage to go out and help me, I might be floating with the fish."

"I overhead Dr. Eddy say that Marshal Parker is coming over to interview you."

"That's right."

"Don't trust the man," Carrie warned. "I think he's involved with all the tragedy that has taken place up on the Comstock Lode."

"You mean with missing stock investors?"

"That's right. Investors as well as the federal officers who have disappeared; my dear father being one of them. I mean to find out what happened to him no matter what the risk or cost. If he's alive, I want to help him. If he's . . ." She choked. "If my father is dead, I want to catch the ones who killed him and make sure that Father's reputation has not been soiled by their deceit and treachery."

Longarm could see the tears welling up in Carrie Lake's pretty green eyes. "Listen," he said, "I've had a real bad day. I'd like to take a little while to sort of get my feet on the ground here before I do anything."

"I can understand that, but you've come to do an investigation and you've already been identified and nearly killed. Marshal, do you really believe that you were taken at gunpoint because you look so terribly prosperous?"

"No," Longarm said. "The man who took me by gunpoint said that he suspected I was a federal officer sent from Denver to investigate what was going on up on the Comstock Lode."

"There you have it," Carrie told him. "You've already been targeted."

"Yes, but not killed," Longarm said. "Did you get a look at the man who put a derringer in my ribs?"

"Only from a distance," she replied. "He was tall and well dressed. When I saw you leaving Virginia Street, I knew that something was very wrong. So I followed hoping that I might be able to learn something and to save your life."

"But you didn't recognize the man?"

"No," Carrie said. "I'd never seen him before but I haven't been here in Reno more than a couple of months so he could be a local person that I just haven't come across."

"Where are you from?"

"San Francisco."

Longarm nodded. "And your father was Marshal Lake?"

"That's right. He was fifty-seven years old and about to

retire with a small, but adequate pension. My mother died about seven years ago and so Father and I have become very close. I didn't want him to come over here because it sounded dangerous and he wasn't really in all that good of health."

"Then why did they send him from the San Francisco office? Why not a younger man?"

"Father was a very intelligent officer and he was incorruptible. They knew that, if he came, he could not be bought or bribed."

"I see."

"Can you help me find him?"

"That's what I came for but this wound is going to set me back a day or two," Longarm admitted.

Carrie stood up and paced back and forth. "It was suggested that we pose as husband and wife. All the other officers came alone and it was felt that . . . well, you needed to look and act differently."

"But they've already identified me."

"Yes, down here in Reno," Carrie said. "But not up in Virginia City. We could still go up there together and . . ."

"No," Longarm interrupted. He softened his voice. "It has nothing to do with you or your father. I just have to work alone."

Carrie stopped pacing and stood very rigid. "I understand what you are saying but you must also understand that I have been here in Reno waiting for you to come and find some answers to questions that I must know. And you also have to realize that I won't just go away. If you go up to Virginia City, I'm coming too. We can pose as a married couple . . . or not. I don't care but I will *not* be left behind."

Longarm could see that nothing he could say would change this beautiful young woman's mind. "All right," he told her. "I can't stop you from going up there but we can't be posing as a husband and wife because they might already know about me and then your life would be in real danger."

"I'm not afraid of what we might find and I'm not one to shrink away and tremble at the first sign of any danger."

Longarm made up his mind. "Carrie, you could be of help to me. Tell you what; let's go up to the Comstock . . . but not together. If you can catch a stage today, then leave at once and when you get to Virginia City, get a room in a good hotel or ladies' boardinghouse. I'll come up tomorrow and we can get in touch but not be seen together."

"But . . . but what should I *do* up there?"

"I have no idea," Longarm told her. "But a beautiful young woman like you should be able to think of something."

"I will," she vowed. "And you won't get killed down here?"

"Nope," Longarm promised. "I'll be there to join you and help find out what happened to your father and the others come hell or high water."

And then Carrie did something surprising. She rushed over to the table where Longarm was resting and kissed him on the cheek.

"For good luck," she said on her way out the door.

Longarm managed a smile as the door closed and said to himself, "A kiss for luck is not a bad thing, especially when it comes from a woman as brave and beautiful as Miss Lake."

Chapter 10

Longarm was bandaged up and preparing to leave Dr.
Eddy's office when a short, bowlegged and barrel-chested
man barged through the front door.

"Doc, I want to speak to that fella that was shot," he demanded. "I hear he's another damned federal marshal."

Longarm heard Dr. Eddy's voice turn cold. "My patient
will be out in a moment."

"Can't wait," he said, pushing past the physician into
the examining room where he confronted Longarm. "Are
you another federal officer?"

"That's right," Longarm told the man as he finished
cleaning the mud off his gun and holster.

"How come you didn't report in to me when you got off
the train!" the man shouted.

"I only report to my own boss in Denver," Longarm answered, taking a strong and immediate dislike to this man
who had outfitted himself to look like Buffalo Bill Cody.
He was dressed in a beaded and fringed leather jacket and
had Cody's trademark mustache and goatee. Parker even
wore leather britches with fringes and they were stuffed
into a fancy pair of tooled leather boots.

"Is that right?" The little town marshal sneered. "Well, I

am the law in Reno, and I don't much appreciate other badge toters comin' into my town and raisin' a ruckus. You killed a man in that river."

"It was self-defense, in case you haven't heard."

"I don't care what it was. You caused me and my deputy a lot of dirty work because now my man has to find and then fish his body out of the water."

"Sounds like your deputy is the one who has to do all the dirty work."

"Don't argue with me."

Longarm took a deep breath and tried to hold back his temper. "Marshal Parker, the man in the river abducted me at gunpoint. He knew I was an officer of the law and I think he meant to kill me."

"Maybe he just wanted your money."

"That's possible," Longarm said, "but I doubt it. From the way he was acting, I think I'm lucky to be just wounded."

Parker studied the bandage. "I take it that you'll survive."

"When you find the body, I want to know who he was and how he knew that I was a law officer."

"You ever been in Reno before?"

"Yes."

"Then that explains it," Parker said. "Someone recognized you."

"It's been quite a while since I visited."

"People have long memories when they think they've been wronged," Parker said. "In our business, we tend to make lasting enemies."

Longarm did not think anyone had recognized him but it was a possibility. "I'm staying at the Regis Hotel. When you find out who the man in the river is, let me know."

"Are you telling me what to do?"

Longarm shoved his gun into his holster and buttoned up his shirt watching Parker's face turned redder by the second. Finally, the man shouted, "Mister, I asked you a damned question!"

Longarm started to push past the man but Parker grabbed his arm and tried to turn him around.

"Mister," he hissed, "I—"

Longarm stomped the heel of his boot down hard on Parker's toe causing the man to cry out in pain and then fall back into a chair. Longarm grabbed Marshal Parker by his goatee and shook his head like he would that of a mischievous billy goat.

"You broke my foot, you big bastard!"

Longarm wasn't listening. "Parker," he warned, "don't you ever lay a hand on me again or the next time I'll break your arm."

The town marshal tried to reach for his gun and Longarm backhanded him across the mouth, splitting his lip. Parker's eyes rolled up in his head and then he swayed and fell down into the doctor's chair.

"How a pompous little fool like you ever got elected to office," Longarm said as he was leaving the doctor's office, "has got to be Reno's *biggest* mystery. Doc?"

Dr. Eddy was speaking to a fat woman who was complaining of shortness of breath. The doctor turned. "Yes?"

"Marshal Parker's foot or some of his toes might be broken."

"Why, he wasn't limping when he arrived. How did that happen?"

"He stepped on my patience and I stepped on his foot," Longarm answered as he was leaving.

Longarm went back to the Regis Hotel and took a hot bath despite the doctor's orders not to get his bandages wet. Getting them wet wasn't a problem because he removed the bandages first. He was so filthy from the river water and mud that he had to get cleaned up, and when that was done he stropped his razor and gave himself a nice, close shave. Studying himself in the mirror and deciding he looked at least half human, he reapplied his bandages, dressed and stepped out into the hallway.

"Room service," he shouted until a clerk appeared.

"I need my suit clothes cleaned and pressed." Longarm gave the man a wad of soggy dollars. "And I want a bottle of your best whiskey brought to this room right away. Oh, and in two hours, a large, rare steak, potatoes and whatever else you can find worth eating."

Longarm gathered his wet and muddy clothing and tossed them on the hallway carpet.

The hotel clerk studied first the pile of clothes and then the soggy wad in his hand, probably trying to guess if there was enough money to pay for everything this big man was ordering. "Anything else?"

"As a matter of fact there is something," Longarm said. "I would like my muddy boots cleaned and polished."

"Yes, sir."

"And keep whatever change is left over."

"Thank you."

Longarm went back to his whiskey and his meditation by the window. He was disturbed to have nearly been killed and mad at himself for being caught off guard. But the thing of it was, he really hadn't expected anyone to know that he was a federal law officer who had just arrived all the way from Denver to investigate the mysterious disappearance of the San Francisco federal officers. So how did the tall pipe-smoking man know he was the law?

Longarm couldn't answer that one. The only explanations that Longarm could think of was that Billy Vail had telegraphed Carrie Lake or Marshal Parker his description in the hope that they might meet him at the train depot and be of some assistance. Either that or someone at the hotel or from the train had tipped the pipe smoker that another federal officer had arrived in Reno.

Either way, the result had almost been fatal.

Longarm was sure that Carrie had not misspoken and given his identity away to the man who'd forced him to the riverbank at gunpoint, and there was no way of knowing about the other explanations.

"I've got to really be on my guard from now on," Longarm told himself. "If all those other federal officers disappeared, then there are people hereabouts who must be very calculating and clever."

Longarm drank some more whiskey because his side was hurting like a bugger. Tomorrow, it would be feeling even worse.

I'll leave for the Comstock the day after tomorrow, he told himself. *But until then, I think I'll lie low and get some rest and try to sort things out a bit so that I don't get into another fix like I did today.*

Chapter 11

The next day, Longarm sent a telegram to Denver asking Billy Vail if he would check and try to verify that Carrie Lake really was related to Marshal Lake. He was sure that she was, but it didn't hurt to make sure. The last line of his telegram read: *Miss Carrie Lake has green eyes and black hair. She said her mother had died some time ago and that her father is/was fifty-seven years old. Can you confirm this information out of San Francisco?*

Longarm sent the telegraph off knowing that he would hear from Billy Vail in a matter of hours, not days. He hadn't seen any point in telling Billy about all his troubles either in Laramie or when he'd nearly been murdered beside the Truckee. Billy could get excitable, and since there was nothing the man could do from Denver, Longarm did not see any reason to put extra strain on his already weak heart.

After sending the telegram, Longarm went to see Dr. Eddy because the man had wanted to check his bullet wound and change the bandages.

"How are you feeling today, Marshal?" the doctor asked.

"I've felt better but I've also felt a lot worse."

"You lost a fair amount of blood," Dr. Eddy told him. "You should be resting quietly for at least a week."

"Not a chance, Doc. I'm heading for the Comstock Lode tomorrow."

"That would be very inadvisable and foolish," the doctor told him. "But then again, I suspect that you have no choice given the disappearance of those San Francisco marshals."

"You know about 'em, huh?"

"Of course. Everyone in Reno and Virginia City knows that some skulduggery is going on."

"Do you have any theories?" Longarm asked.

"Not really. I think that there has always been an enormous amount of corruption taking place on the Comstock Lode in regard to its wildly fluctuating stock market." The doctor shrugged. "I never could understand why, when it came to gold and silver, people just plain lose their good sense. I mean, in any other enterprise, investors are usually prudent. But the idea of buying some stock based on the unlikely possibility of finding a new vein of pure ore seems to me the riskiest of undertakings."

"And yet," Longarm reminded the man, "intelligent people contract gold fever every bit as easily as stupid people."

"I know that to be true," Dr. Eddy said. "I've known bankers, lawyers, doctors and even professional geologists to throw caution to the wind and buy vastly overvalued mining stocks. How can you explain it?"

"Gold fever," Longarm stated. "It was like that over in the Sierras and it's the same mentality here in Nevada. I've seen it happen plenty of times in Colorado. It's my opinion that when men see gold they most likely will lose all their reason."

"Strange, isn't it?" Dr. Eddy mused. "Have you ever been stricken hard with gold fever?"

Longarm had to grin. "As a matter of fact, I have. When I was a young man there was a small gold strike back in

West Virginia where I grew up. Nothing like we have out in the West, but even so it caused otherwise intelligent men to drop everything and hurry off to the hills with a crazed look in their eyes. Farmers left their crops to rot in the fields, merchants closed their stores, sailors jumped ship and raced to the hills. And I was right there among 'em, my poor mind as frenzied as popcorn in a skillet."

Dr. Eddy grinned with self-deprecation. "Truth be known, I've often thought I should have opened my practice up on the Comstock and dabbled in the market. But my fine wife, Cora Lee, is repelled by the riotous life up there and refused to even consider living in Virginia City, Gold Hill or Silver City. And I have four children so I stayed here in Reno and I've done rather well. But maybe . . . maybe had I gone up the mountain and joined that craziness when the Comstock was really at its pinnacle of production . . . then I might have wound up as rich as John McKay or Sandy Bowers who now owns a mansion out in Washoe Valley."

"More likely you'd have wound up a man without a home, your health or your family," Longarm told the physician.

"I suppose. I'm not complaining, but sometimes in life a man likes to toss caution aside and boldly leap for the golden ring, so to speak. Do you understand me, Marshal?"

"Of course."

"I sometimes get tired of people being sick and complaining. A lot of them have ailments that exist only in their minds. Even very healthy old people get bored and want sympathy so they invent their maladies. Believe in them until they actually happen."

Longarm didn't understand. "You mean a person can get sick if they tell themselves they are sick for a long while?"

"That's what I'm saying," Dr. Eddy admitted. "You see, the mind and body are far more closely connected than you and I suspect. A whining, negative person who is always fretting and fussing will put themselves into poor health. I've seen it happen too often. Other people just seem to make the best of things and keep busy. Almost always, they have the strongest constitutions and the least amount of sickness."

"Maybe they are prayin' folks whose prayers are being answered by God."

Eddy shrugged. "I can't say about that although I do know that prayer can work miracles. But whether or not it is God doing the miracle or the hope and faith of the individual that makes the change, I'm not prepared to say. And I do pray when I'm in the worst of fixes. I'm just not sure if it ever works or not, and I don't expect to ever see a burning bush or an angel on my shoulder."

The doctor finished his bandaging. "Marshal Long, I have to tell you that I've never seen a human body with so many scars. Have you considered changing occupations?"

"Never. I like what I do," Longarm answered.

"Do you have a wife and children? A home and hearth?"

"Nope. I live alone in a cramped and cluttered apartment in Denver. I don't like to cook so I mainly eat out."

"Think you'll ever get married? It's a wonderful institution, you know."

"I might," Longarm said. "I'm going to think real hard about it as soon as I hit sixty. As for having children, well, they are fine when they get older but the young ones give me headaches. I don't much care for babies, Doc. I know that sounds awful, but that's the truth of it."

"Don't feel ashamed. Women usually love babies but most of us men can't really stand them. We just . . . just tolerate the squalling, crapping little buggers."

Longarm laughed. He hadn't expected that kind of candor, but he appreciated and respected this man and said, "If I get shot again up on the Comstock Lode and I'm not leaking too badly, I'll have them load me up on a stage and run me down here so you can patch me up again."

"Just stay out of harm's way."

"I'm afraid that's impossible because five marshals are missing and someone might want to make me number six," Longarm said.

"What are you going to do different than the others in order not to share their uncertain fate?"

"Damned if I know."

As he was leaving, Dr. Eddy stepped outside and said in a low voice, "Trust no one up there. I *mean* that, Marshal."

"That's good advice, Doc. I'll put it in practice."

"And don't lose any more blood!" Eddy shouted as Longarm headed back to the telegraph office.

"Here it is," the operator said, handing Longarm the telegraph. "Be one dollar."

Longarm paid the man and took the telegram outside to read. Billy Vail's answer was short and to the point, which bespoke of his intense dislike to waste money. *Your questions about Miss Lake are all confirmed. Green eyes, black hair and twenty-six years old. Father was fifty-seven years old and well-liked by all. Mother died ten years ago of cancer. Be careful and stay in closer touch. B. Vail*

"Fair enough," Longarm said to himself as he headed back to the Regis. "Miss Lake is legitimate. But the pipe-smoker knew I was a federal marshal. I wonder if Marshal Parker and his deputy have found the man's body and gotten any identification. Think I'll pay them a visit before I go back to the hotel."

When Longarm walked into Marshal Parker's office, the marshal was not present but his deputy was reading a cheap dime novel whose cover depicted a glorified Buffalo Bill surrounded by wild and attacking Indians. Just Cody all alone with a gun in each fist fighting it out to a glorious end.

"Those dime novels excite you?" Longarm asked the deputy.

The man's cheeks colored with embarrassment. "I enjoy 'em and so does Marshal Parker. Anything wrong with that?"

"Not at all, as long as you don't believe what you read."

"Marshal Parker says Buffalo Bill Cody was the fastest man with a gun who ever lived."

Longarm declined to reply.

"Well?"

"Well what?"

"What do you say about Buffalo Bill?"

Longarm was honest. "William Fredrick Cody is one of the finest marksmen I've ever seen with either a gun or a rifle."

"You've *seen* him shoot?" The deputy's voice betrayed his sudden excitement.

"Sure," Longarm said. "Cody has won many shooting contests in Colorado. Even more impressive, he took part in over a dozen Indian fights, mostly against the Cheyenne and the Sioux. He's a brave man and deserves his fame, but he's not at all a fast-draw specialist."

"The hell you say!" The deputy looked as if he had been personally insulted by this remark.

Longarm didn't care what the deputy thought but the man needed some enlightenment. "Out in the open field I'd say Cody was as deadly a man as anyone could face because he is fearless and accurate. But in close quarters, like in a saloon . . . well, the man I'd most fear is John Wesley Hardin, who lives mostly down in Texas. I know for a fact he has gunned down more than twenty men in stand-up fights, not from ambush or behind."

"Never heard of the man. Any dime novels been written on this Hardin fella?"

"Not yet but I'm sure there will be."

"I'd rather read about Buffalo Bill and Wild Bill Hickok. That Hardin fella can't be much if we haven't even heard of him."

"Not many people this far west have," Longarm said. "But he's as deadly a man as ever strapped on a gun, and whether you believe it or not, he'd kill Bill Cody in the blink of an eye."

"Oh bullshit!" the deputy said, waving the dime novel overhead. "Buffalo Bill would ventilate that Hardin fella before he could even clear leather."

Longarm was tired of the conversation. "I'm here to find out who the man was that put a bullet in my side. Did you find his body in the river and identify him?"

"Oh, they found his body all right. Only it had been swept over so many river rocks that there wasn't much left of his face. River rocks beat and scraped his nose clean off and all the flesh on his face was gone. Maybe some of them big trout or catfish had a feed on his soggy body. I don't know, and I don't even want to think about it."

To make his point, the deputy shivered and grimaced.

"But were there no papers or anything on his person that would tell us who he was?"

"Not a thing," the deputy said looking almost pleased. "But, if you don't believe me, go on over to the undertaker's office and have a look at what's left of the man. He's all bloated up and he'll turn your stomach unless it's made of cast iron."

Longarm saw that there were dozens of dime novels on a nearby table and when he went over and looked at them, most were highly romanticized tales about Buffalo Bill Cody.

"You want to come back tomorrow when Marshal Parker is here?"

"Maybe I'll do that," Longarm said, not particularly interested in telling this man or his boss that he would be on his way to the Comstock Lode bright and early tomorrow morning.

Longarm didn't care to go to the undertaker's office. He knew what the man had looked like, but he'd hoped for a name.

Now, even that seemed out of the question.

Chapter 12

Longarm checked out of the Regis Hotel the next morning. He wasn't feeling in tip-top shape, but he'd do all right unless forced into a hard fistfight. Dr. Eddy had told him that, unless he did something really stupid and strenuous, the wound was not likely to tear open and start hemorrhaging.

The Virginia City & Gold Hill Stagecoach Line charged two dollars a head to take a passenger up to the Comstock, which was located about thirty miles to the southeast and clung to the slopes of barren Sun Mountain. Longarm was dismayed to discover that the eight A.M. coach was sold out and that he'd have to wait for a second coach that did not depart Reno for two more hours.

"Damn," he muttered. "I shouldn't have had that second cup of coffee."

"Me neither," a middle-aged gentleman said, overhearing Longarm. "I expect we ought to get tickets right now or we might even lose our seats on the next stage up to the Comstock Lode."

"Good idea," Longarm agreed, following the man to the ticket counter.

"Good morning, Mr. Hammond," the ticket agent said

with a toothy grin. "Going up the mountain again today on business?"

"Yes," Hammond said, removing and polishing his thick gold-rimmed spectacles. "Our bank has to make a decision today on the purchase of a new mining stock being issued."

"I hope it's a good 'un," the agent said.

"You never know. I'll be meeting with our geologist and assayer to make the final determination. Probably have to stay up there for three or four days. I'd rather be here in Reno where there is considerable more civility."

"Yeah," the ticket agent said, taking the banker's payment and issuing a ticket. "I hear it's still pretty wild and woolly up there."

"That," Hammond replied, "is a nice way of phrasing it."

Longarm was next and he bought his ticket. That done, he saw the banker head up the street, probably to wait in his office until the next stage departed.

Longarm had nowhere to wait but he was allowed to check in his small baggage, so he walked back down Virginia Street to the bridge. Same retired minister was there fretting and fussing over what he considered the lewd behavior of the Truckee River ducks.

Not interested in striking up another conversation with the man, Longarm crossed the bridge and went down to the riverbank where he sat under a tree and watched the water flow. The Truckee, he knew, originated from Lake Tahoe, one of the deepest and most beautiful mountain lakes Longarm had ever visited. It was high and cool up there in the tall Ponderosa Pines, and Longarm would have liked nothing better than to have taken the Union Pacific on up into the Sierras and rested for a week or two and maybe caught some fish in Lake Tahoe. The fishing up there was exceptional, and because of the water's famed clarity and coldness, the meat of fish from the lake was firm and tasty.

Longarm wandered around town for awhile and was

about to turn back and head for the stage when Marshal Parker hailed him from across Virginia Street.

"Damn," Longarm muttered, not interested in meeting or talking with the lawman.

Parker hurried across the street. "I wanted to tell you that the man who shot you was too battered to be recognized by the time we dragged him out of the river about ten miles south of town. You need to come to my office and write out a full description."

"Maybe later," Longarm stalled.

"No, right now."

Longarm didn't want to reveal that he was going up to Virginia City so he said, "I am feeling a little punk and heading back to my hotel room. I'll stop by your office as soon as I'm feeling up to it."

"Won't take ten damned minutes!"

"Sorry," Longarm said as he turned on his heel and left the arrogant lawman in his wake, "but it *will* have to wait."

Longarm had the feeling that Parker was watching, perhaps even following him so it seemed an intelligent move to go into the Regis, then slip out the back and hurry on to the stage station. And that is what he did to avoid letting Parker know that he was leaving Reno.

Back at the stagecoach line offices, Longarm was happy to see that the ten o'clock coach was only half filled. The banker, Hammond, was already seated and reading some papers that he'd taken from his briefcase.

"Hello again," Longarm said, easing himself up into the coach and trying not to wince with pain.

"Oh, hello. My name is Arnold Hammond. And yours?"

Longarm shook the banker's extended hand, finding it soft as expected. The man himself, however, looked reasonably fit.

Two more passengers boarded the stagecoach, what looked to be a down-on-his-luck gambler who smelled like he badly needed a bath, and a chubby prostitute who had a double chin and enormous breasts. Despite being quite hefty, she was attractive, expensively dressed and quite cheerful. Most prostitutes, Longarm had discovered, were rather introverted and surly when not with a customer or trying to lure one to hand over money.

"My name is Izzy," she announced to the three men while lifting her chin slightly. "And I'm working at the Silver Slipper Hotel and Saloon. If you gentlemen come to visit me, I'll buy you a free drink and then I'll show you a good time."

The gambler was a dissipated-looking, smallish fellow with deep-set, wary eyes and a pointy chin. He grinned showing a badly sculpted gold tooth. "And my name is Chauncy Maxwell," he announced rather grandly considering his clothes were in desperate need of cleaning. "At your service, Miss Izzy."

"It's short for Isabella," the prostitute explained. "Doesn't sound so uppity, either." Izzy looked sideways at Longarm, her eyes lingering on his face. "And your name?"

"Custis Long."

"I couldn't help but notice you've suffered an injury to your side."

"It's nothing serious."

"I hope not. Have you seen a doctor?"

"Yes and he said that I should just take it a little easy for awhile."

"Well, Mr. Long," Izzy said, "If you don't mind my asking, what is your business on the Comstock?"

"I'm an investor," Longarm told her. "Not a big one, but I have heard that there have been some new discoveries up there, and I thought the Comstock Lode might not be entirely played out yet and that there might be an interesting and unusual investment opportunity."

"Oh, I see," Izzy purred. "Well, I could sure tell you some stories about those mines. The Ophir. The Consolidated Virginia. The California. Those were the biggest ones and they made up what was called The Big Bonanza. But they're all played out now. Flooded and abandoned."

The banker, Hammond, interrupted to say, "That is true. Those early mines were bonanzas and made millions for their investors. But the Comstock Lode is riddled with small mines and some of them are being reopened again and worked very profitably."

Longarm didn't know much about deep, hard-rock mining. "I understood that the silver and gold veins run very deep and are difficult to reach."

"That is very true," the banker said. "The Ophir Mine, for example, was nearly four thousand feet deep before the heat and scalding water finally forced it to shut down. Same with many of the other big mines that had huge engines pumping water and pushing down fresh air to the work crews. But there are smaller mines that are now starting to generate some excitement."

"So I've heard," Longarm said.

"How much money do you plan to invest?" the gambler bluntly asked, naked greed showing in his beady eyes.

Longarm turned to stare at the man. "That is not a smart question for any investor to answer and it's a rude one for any stranger to ask."

"Don't make any difference to me," the gambler said, his eyes sliding away. "I was just trying to carry on a conversation."

Longarm turned away from Chauncy Maxwell, which was, he was certain, an alias. "I'm not even close to being rich," he told Izzy and Hammond, "but I have recently sold a sizable cattle ranch in the Denver area and now have the means to investigate opportunities."

"Why on earth did you leave Colorado and a cattle ranch?" Izzy asked. "I hear it's real pretty there and cattle ranching is a nicer business than hard-rock mining."

"I like new adventures," Longarm told her. "Ranching became a bore and I wanted to try something different and more exciting. Also, this high desert country is drier, which is easier on my joints."

Longarm clenched and unclenched his big fists to illustrate his point.

Izzy winked, her eyes dropping to his crotch. "I can work the stiffness out of your *best* joint, Mr. Long. I can do it in ways that you might not even be able to imagine."

Her proposition was so frank and unexpected that Longarm felt a little embarrassed, and from the look on the banker's face, he was not the only one caught by surprise. The gambler, however, was not at all embarrassed and proved himself a coarse man when he said, "When we get to Virginia City, how much will you charge to suck the stiffness out of *my* best joint?"

Izzy was obviously a high-class prostitute who didn't appreciate the gambler's crude inference or lecherous manner. "I think you'd be better off finding a pig to suck your joint, Mr. Maxwell. Because if it smells as rank as the rest of you, only a pig would touch your joint and then only if you dipped it in a jar of sweet jam."

Longarm exploded with laughter. The banker tried not to smile while the gambler, Chauncy Maxwell, burned with indignation and hatred. When the laughter died, he hissed, "Izzy, I'll recoup my fortunes and pay you a visit at the Silver Slipper. And when I do, I'll put you down on your knees and . . ."

Longarm grabbed Maxwell by the throat, cutting off his acid words in mid-sentence and causing the gambler's eyes to bulge with terror. "Don't say another word," Longarm softly warned. "Not one more word for the rest of this trip up to the Comstock."

Chauncy Maxwell managed to nod and Longarm released his hold. Izzy beamed and leaned close to whisper in Longarm's ear. "I love a man who stands up for a woman's honor. Even a fallen woman like myself."

"My pleasure," Longarm said.

"It will be my pleasure to serve you tonight for free, and I'm not talking about just a drink, Mr. Long."

The banker and the gambler overheard Izzy's offer and they turned their faces away, the banker no doubt mortified.

Longarm nodded to Izzy indicating that he might just accept her generous offer and then he, too, turned his face to the passing scenery.

The road up to the Comstock was as crooked as a southwestern sidewinder. Built at enormous cost in the early 1860s, it had once been continuously clogged with miners and commerce as the Comstock Lode gained worldwide fame and experienced deep-rock miners rushed to its call from as far away as Australia and Wales. Today, most of the Comstock Lode's still considerable commerce was carried by the V&T Railroad, which ran from Carson City up through Silver City and Gold Hill to Virginia City.

"It's a terribly rugged, tough and dry country, isn't it, Mr. Long?" the banker said as they eased through another hairpin turn and continued on up the perilously steep grade. "But the views are tremendous."

"Indeed they are," Longarm said as they slowly climbed more than two thousand feet up from the Washoe Valley floor, which was green and dotted by small farms. Across the Washoe Valley were the towering eastern slopes of the mighty Sierra Nevada Mountains. They looked gray-green in the midday sun and some of the highest peaks were covered by patches of shimmering snow.

"Can you imagine," Hammond said, "the placer miners of California, accustomed to the green pines and beautiful mountain meadows coming over here in 1859 to try and strike their fortunes on the Comstock Lode?"

"What do you mean?" Longarm asked.

"I mean that the Forty-Niners were accustomed to the lush beauty of the western Sierras, and they were also probably expecting to be able to continue their placer mining in rivers, creeks and streams. But when they crossed

99

over those Sierras and saw these awful, barren hills and mountains with almost no trees save the pinions and the junipers they must have thought they were being delivered into hell."

"Hell?" Longarm asked.

"Because these mountains have no water. No rivers or streams but instead only stinking seeps. And worst of all, they would no longer be able to work out in the healthy sunlight with a pick and a pan where every man is the equal of every other. No, sir! Instead, they would have to be employees of huge companies and go down to unheard of depths under Sun Mountain where the heat and poisonous gasses burn a man's lungs. Where the single misplaced strike of a miner's pick could bring a torrent of scalding water boiling them alive like lobster in a cook's kettle."

Longarm nodded with understanding. "I hadn't thought of that, Mr. Hammond. But you're right. It must have been quite a shock to the early California miners to have to come over here and do a completely different and not so pleasant type of hard-rock mining."

"Oh, it was!" Hammond said convincingly. "My father was one of those early Forty-Niners, and he told me stories of how hard it was here on the Comstock Lode. He was one of the first men to help found a Miner's Union and they demanded—and won—the right to earn three dollars a day."

"For a fact?"

"For a fact," Hammond said proudly. "That was an unheard of amount of money to pay a common miner back when the Civil War was raging in the east. But the death count in the mines was so high and the working conditions so hellish that the union prevailed and that wage was won. And you know what, Mr. Long?"

"What?"

"Three dollars a day is *still* what the miners are receiving up here . . . when they can find a job."

Longarm shook his head. "I wouldn't be a hard-rock

miner for five times that amount a day. The idea of going down four or five hundred feet—or even more—suspended in a cage by a wire cable into that awful heat and darkness sends shivers up my spine."

"Mr. Long, if you come by the Silver Slipper tonight, *I'll* send shivers up your spine and other parts of your body as well," Izzy said, giggling.

Longarm glanced down at Izzy's magnificent creamy mounds and thought he might just do that.

"Mr. Long," the banker said, "may I offer a suggestion as to how you might proceed when we reach Virginia City?"

"I would welcome your suggestions."

"Take things slow," Hammond said gravely. "Invest in nothing until you have actually seen the mine whose stock you are considering as an investment."

"Will they allow that?"

"Of course they will!" the banker exclaimed. "And, if they won't, then cross that mine and its stock off your list of possibilities. Also, look at reports that tell you at least a five-year history of the mine's most recent production and the purity of its ore. It's not all the same. And ask at what depth the latest ore is being taken."

"Why?"

The banker smiled tolerantly. "Because even if the mine is producing high-quality ore, if the production costs are too high, then the mine will eventually go out of business."

"That makes sense," Longarm replied.

"Of course it does," Hammond continued. "There is no doubt that there are still huge pockets of gold and silver to be discovered under Sun Mountain, but at what extraction costs? And also look at management and capitalization. A poorly managed mine or one that does not have the capital to invest in machinery or exploration is going to fail."

Longarm was impressed by Arnold Hammond's knowledge and advice. But then, that was what this man did for a living. He studied the mining stock and made recommendations to his bank. He was an expert.

"Mr. Hammond, do you mind if I ask you what particular mines you are looking at on this trip?"

The banker smiled and shook his head. "I wish I could divulge that information, but I cannot."

"I understand," Longarm said, thinking he might just keep an eye on this gentleman banker and watch which mining properties he visited.

"There's the summit," Izzy called, sticking her head out the window. "And just beyond is the Queen of the Comstock Lode, dear Virginia City."

Longarm said, "Do you like it up here?"

"Like it?" Izzy asked. "The truth is that I love Virginia City and can't get her out of my blood."

"Why?"

"Well," Izzy told him, "when I first came here, I was slimmer and prettier but very young and stupid. I made a lot of dumb mistakes. But living up here was exciting and a great education. I met poor men and watched a few of them become millionaires. I saw millionaires become beggars, and I watched the town burn down four times! I met Samuel Clemens, who worked as a poor reporter on the *Territorial Enterprise* long before becoming famous as Mark Twain. I've seen Virginia City at its best and worst but she always came back and I'm betting that she will again."

"Is that so?" the gambler sullenly dared to ask.

"It is," Izzy answered, "because I've just bought the Silver Slipper Hotel and Saloon, lock, stock and barrel. She is where I first worked and now I own her."

Longarm was impressed and, from what he read on the banker's face as well as that of the gambler, so were they.

A few minutes later, Izzy let out a howl of pure delight and stuck her head out the window again. "There she is, gents!"

Longarm looked out the window to see Virginia City. The famous mining town was still impressive. Cradled on the eastern slope of the barren Sun Mountain, she huddled like a proud old dowager. He could see the silver-tipped spires of a church and the great saloons, Piper's Opera House and other impressive buildings that were now slowly falling into disrepair.

Would Virginia City once again become a magnet for the world's deep-rock miners and fortune seekers? Had she indeed given up everything she had to offer and was now just fading into history?

Longarm hoped not. And then he looked to the east and saw the vast cemeteries. One for Catholics only. Another for Chinese, Indians and Mexicans. Another, the largest of all, for the thousands of miners who had died of rock falls, mining disasters and murders.

Longarm stared long and hard at the great mining town because it was stark and it was decaying but it was, in its own way, sadly still magnificent.

Chapter 13

Longarm checked into a highly recommended boarding-house called the Pink Mansion, which was now a hotel. His room was elegant and he knew it must have cost a small fortune to have furnished it in Virginia City's glory days. His room was at least three hundred square feet and illuminated by a crystal chandelier that would have done any home in Denver proud, and the furniture was hand-carved, imported from Italy and very heavy. The floor was polished oak topped with a huge Persian rug and the drapes, once a deep blue velvet, were now badly faded. Longarm's room had its own bath, piano, massive armoire and private entry to a little balcony that faced Sun Mountain. He could leave or enter his room at any hour without being noticed.

Longarm had chosen the Pink Mansion on the recommendation of Arnold Hammond the Reno banker who Longarm supposed was already engaged in his business meetings.

That evening Longarm enjoyed a superb dinner served by a wizened Chinaman while in the company of the Pink Mansion's handsome young owners, Mr. and Mrs. Herbert Gordon. In the face of hard times, it was clear that the Gordons were doing their best to hang on to their once magnif-icent mansion, formerly owned by a mining millionaire.

"I hope you enjoyed your supper and will be staying with us for at least a few days," Gordon said. He was well-dressed and although he seemed confident, Longarm noticed that the man's fingernails were bitten to the quick. "Cecilia and I very much want all our guests to be comfortable and to return to the Pink Mansion whenever possible. We want you to feel as comfortable as if you were in your own home."

"That's very gracious of you," Longarm said as he was being served tea by the expressionless old Chinaman.

"My compliments to your Chinese cook because the meal was excellent," Longarm told the Gordons. "And I will be staying for several days while I educate myself on the future of the mines here on the Comstock Lode. If I like what I learn, I'll probably make some mining investments."

"How exciting!" Cecilia Gordon exclaimed, tossing her auburn hair and giving Longarm a dazzling smile. "And while we know that the Comstock mines will never again produce as they did twenty years ago, we're sure that there is about to be a *huge* resurgence and it's a smart man who invests when the stock prices are currently so low. Isn't that right, Herbert, dear?"

"Oh, most certainly so!" the man said with far more en-thusiasm than the remark called for. "Now is definitely the time to invest."

"Good to hear it," Longarm told them. "But I'll have to be very cautious because I really don't know much about mining."

"Well," Gordon said, "I just happen to have been a min-ing engineer."

"Is that right?" Longarm was wondering why the man was no longer employed in that capacity. And from the sense of things, it looked like the Gordons could sure use money. "What do you do now?"

"I . . . ah . . . well, both Cecelia and I stay pretty busy fixing up this place. It was in rough shape when we bought it last year. And I sure never realized how expensive it is to keep up a place like this. Why, our winter heating costs alone are—"

"Herbert," Cecelia said, "I'm sure that Mr. Long is not interested in our heating bill."

"Oh, yes. Of course not." Herbert Gordon looked embarrassed and started to bite his fingernails but caught himself in time.

"My husband," the lovely young woman said, "was employed by the Comstock Mining Company, one of the largest and most respected in Virginia City. But they pulled out of the business about two years ago and so we've been fortunate to have gotten into this lovely old mansion and entertaining guests like you, Mr. Long."

"That's right," Gordon said quickly. "We really are enjoying it. But I am my own boss now and do have a little extra time when needed. So, if you're interested, I'd be happy to tell you what mines and which areas I think are ripe for the smart investor to make a killing."

"That's good of you," Longarm told him as he sipped his tea. "I'd be grateful to hear your thoughts and suggestions."

"How much money, if you don't mind my asking, are you prepared to invest?" Cecilia asked with a wide and disarming smile. "It's important for Herbert to have some idea before he talks about various properties. Isn't that right, dear?"

"It is," Herbert readily agreed. "But, of course, if that's—"

"Five thousand dollars," Longarm said, without giving the figure much thought. "Yes, that would be my investment, and while I know that it's not a great deal of money, I hope—given the depressed prices you spoke of—that it would be enough to reap a sizable profit."

"Most certainly!" Cecilia cried, her eyes round with excitement. "I'm sure that you could buy up . . . well, an entire mine and all its machinery for that much money."

"I'd say that's true," Herbert agreed. "But it would, of course, be one of the smaller mines. I happen to know some properties that would fit very nicely into that price range."

The man winked. "Some real *sleepers*."

Longarm now understood perfectly that this young, somewhat desperate couple was eyeing him more as a potential savior than as a mere guest that they would help out. And while he didn't know where this was leading, he decided to play along.

"I would," Longarm said, "insist on paying you a consulting fee."

"No!" Gordon cried, throwing up his hands as if he would not dream of touching money. "I'd be happy to help you as a friend and as our guest."

"How very generous," Longarm said looking as dumb as a post. "But I'd insist."

"Well, Mr. Long, in that case," Cecilia told him, "if you really would feel more comfortable with that arrangement we would be pleased."

Herbert was beaming. "You know, Mr. Long, in their heyday, our most profitable mines such as the Ophir sold stock by the running foot at unbelievable prices."

"But now," the wife said, "they're almost giving the stock away so your timing is perfect, Mr. Long."

"That's good to hear," Longarm told them.

"We'll go out and I'll show you some properties first thing tomorrow morning," Herbert promised. "If that would be all right?"

"Sure," Longarm told the man, figuring that there was little to lose and that Herbert, despite his true mercenary motives, could not help but be of some educational value.

Longarm finished his tea and excused himself.

"You're probably tired after that awful coach ride up from Reno," Cecilia said. "And you want to retire early."

"Actually," Longarm told her, "it's a nice evening so I think I'll walk into town and look around. I haven't been up here for many years."

"Not much excitement up here anymore. Just some saloons and gambling houses that rarely have any real entertainment," the young woman said, looking disappointed.

"Now, dear," her husband said, trying to hold a grin, "we really shouldn't be telling our guests what they should do while visiting, should we?"

Cecilia shot her husband a withering glance and he bent his face into his cup of tea. Longarm excused himself and went to his room. Ten minutes later, he was walking up the street into the center of Virginia City.

He passed the *Territorial Enterprise* newspaper office, the Bucket of Blood Saloon and the famous Lucky Dollar noting that the town looked mostly deserted and in a state of rapid decay. The wooden sidewalks were cracked and had missing planks and the business signs were all crying for fresh paint.

Still, Longarm could hear the tinkle of pianos coming from inside a few of the still operating saloons, and when he stopped in front of the Silver Slipper, he heard what he was sure was Izzy's voice singing an old Irish favorite called "The Girl from Shannon Town."

Longarm entered the Silver Slipper and saw that there were perhaps twenty patrons seated at tables playing poker or just watching Izzy sing and do a little soft shoe. The piano was definitely out of tune but no one really cared, and as Longarm ordered a beer, he turned and saw that Izzy had recognized him.

"Come on over here and enjoy the show!" she called, motioning Longarm to a nearby table.

He went to the table and sat. Next thing he knew, Izzy

was in his lap, singing a rousing new song and hugging his neck. Longarm was not a man who liked being the center of attention but he had to admit that he was enjoying Izzy and her exuberance. Besides that she had a nice voice and those big mounds of breast were pushing right up into his face. What the other customers could not see was that Izzy was also wiggling her bottom on his lap, and Longarm was feeling a powerful response.

More beer was brought to him and Izzy sang some of the old favorite songs like: "Little Old Sod Shanty," "Sweet Sierra Sue" and "Dakota Land".

Most of the male customers, Longarm noticed, were middle-aged miners and businesspeople, but a few were old men who appeared to be in their seventies and even eighties.

Izzy's singing and rubbing went on for about three beers and then Longarm could hardly stand the aching in his loins. He leaned in close to those big breasts, inhaled deeply and whispered, "Izzy, I'm getting pretty hot under your dress."

She pretended that she didn't hear him, but when her song was over, she kissed Longarm on the mouth and purred, "I'm getting pretty hot myself, Big Boy. Let's take a short break."

"How short?"

"Long enough Mr. Long," she said with a wink as she patted the piano player on the head and started up a staircase with her caboose wagging like the tail of a mare in heat.

Longarm went right up the stairs after Izzy and that brought a cheer from the aging crowd. "Not exactly private around here, is it," he commented.

Izzy opened the door to what was obviously her living room, bedroom and office. It was crowded with memorabilia, mostly pictures of Virginia City when it was booming. There was even a photograph of Mark Twain, and under it in a special place, was an autographed copy of his famous work *Roughing It*, which had been published in 1872 to great acclaim.

"Your own autographed copy, huh?" Longarm said with admiration.

"Yes, Samuel Clemens was a favorite of mine and I well remember what a greenhorn he was when he first arrived in Virginia City. But he quickly caught the spirit of the town and became quite the celebrity along with his elegant friend, Dan DeQuille. They were quite the pair when they were in the cups, and no two men ever covered a boom-town with more humor."

"I've read *Roughing It* a couple of times and I'll probably end up reading it a couple more," Longarm admitted. "Twain's lively descriptions of Virginia City and other places are unforgettable. I remember that he thought Lake Tahoe so intoxicating with its beauty that vacationing there for three months, 'would restore an Egyptian mummy.'"

Izzy laughed and began to undress while Longarm read a few favorite passages from the famous book aloud. When he finished reading, Izzy was stark naked and reclining on her bed in a position that left no doubt as to what she wanted.

"You don't mess around with a lot of preliminaries, do you?" Longarm said, unbuttoning his coat and vest then removing his gun and boots.

"If you taste as good as you look," she said, "why should I be patient?"

Longarm finished undressing. Izzy said, "That wound of yours looks kinda awful. Are you sure you're not going to hurt yourself, if we get a little wild during the act of lovemaking?"

"Nope," Longarm said. "I can handle whatever you have to offer."

"We'll see." Izzy rolled him onto the bed and then took his manhood in her mouth. "Yummm!"

She worked on him for a long time and it was sheer torture, or pleasure, whichever a man would want to call it. And then Izzy gave him her beautiful breasts to enjoy for awhile before she rolled over and guided his rod into her hot sweetness.

Longarm and Izzy went at each other like starving miners would a Thanksgiving turkey. They were loud, sloppy and lusty. There was no finesse with Izzy. What she wanted was pure, frantic pleasure and Longarm forgot about the soreness in his side and gave the saloon owner all she wanted and more.

When they both started shouting with pleasure, Longarm shot his pork sausage as deep as it would go and emptied his sack until it was as dry as desert sand. Izzy took a moment or two longer, and when she exploded, she nearly bucked Longarm into the ceiling.

"Oh my gosh!" Izzy wheezed, sweating and panting. "You *are* as good as you look. I can sure pick 'em, that's for certain!"

"Glad you are pleased and well satisfied."

"I want more but I have to go down there and sing for my customers. Do you want to come or would you rather wait right here for me to come back up to the room?"

"You'd trust me alone with an autographed copy of *Roughing It*, which is worth a small fortune?"

"Of course I would. You're not no thief."

"You don't know me."

"I trust my judgment about men and know you're a good one. But I wouldn't let that lowlife Chauncy Maxwell alone in this room for a minute because he'd steal me blind."

"I'm going out to look at some mining properties with Herbert Gordon tomorrow morning. Do you know the man?"

"I'm afraid so," Izzy replied.

"What's the problem?"

"Herbert and his wife, Cecelia, aren't to be trusted.

112

They've not been on the Comstock all that long, but they've already been involved in some shady business transactions. Herbert got fired from his job and now the couple is desperately attempting to hang on to the Pink Mansion. They've sunk all their cash into that monstrosity and it's taking them down like a ship plunging toward the bottom of the ocean."

"Sorry to hear that."

"It happens all the time up here. So you be careful and hang on to your money tight."

"I will," Longarm promised.

"And be careful if you go down in any of those old mines. The timbers are rotting and none of them are safe. Not that they ever were safe but they are even less so now that they've been neglected for years and years."

"I'll be careful."

"Herbert Gordon is not a bad man," Izzy said. "Actually, he's kind of sweet and he's doing any menial job around town that he can find to help them keep up appearances. Frankly, I think he's about to have a mental breakdown and that doesn't surprise me."

"Why? Because of their financial strains?"

"That and his wife, who is definitely a man-hater."

"Do you think so?"

"I know so," Izzy said. "Just be careful what you do and say around her. I think she's looking for a way out of that fix that doesn't include her poor husband."

Longarm said, "Thanks for the warning."

"Will you come around tomorrow?"

"I don't know," he said. "I've got a lot to do."

"Well, you know what I've got for you when you do come back," Izzy said with a wiggle and a wink.

Longarm smiled because he *did* know.

Chapter 14

Longarm was sleeping hard in his own bed at the Pink Mansion when he heard a faint but insistent knocking at his private door that opened toward Sun Mountain.

He sat up and reached for his Colt, then tiptoed in his nightshirt over to the door. "Who is it?"

"Carrie. Open up."

Longarm opened the door and there stood Carrie Lake with her arms folded across her bosom and wearing a look of pure exasperation. "Well, well," she said, "if it isn't Romeo himself. Are you alone, or are you enjoying a second woman tonight?"

"I'm alone," Longarm said, "but I was sound asleep and don't appreciate being awakened at this hour. What hour is it, anyway?"

"I had to wait until one o'clock and you were finished with Miss Isabella," the woman snapped. "I've been cooling my heels all evening."

"What is it that you couldn't wait until morning to tell me?"

She didn't answer his question. "Can I come in or must I stand out here in the cold until tomorrow morning?"

Longarm could tell that the woman was out of sorts and

he wasn't too happy himself as he stepped aside and let her enter his room.

"Not bad," she said. "I'm staying at Miss Mabel's Boardinghouse and you're staying at a damned mansion. How do you federal officers rate?"

Longarm went over to one of the felt-covered easy chairs and plopped down in his nightshirt. "Why don't you get to the point of this meeting before I grab you by the hair and toss you out into the sagebrush?"

"You speak to me that way? The person who saved you from being drowned in the Truckee River?"

Longarm could see her point. "All right," he said, yawning. "I think we need to start all over. Good evening, Miss Lake! How are you tonight and what can I do for you?"

"Good evening to you, Mr. Long. What you can do for me is to be more careful who you consort with. Miss Izzy is not what I expected of you on your very first night in Virginia City."

"I learned some things from her."

"Yeah, I'll just bet you did. But did you learn anything about who killed my father and the others?"

"Not yet."

"And you won't. At least, not from that woman. So what are you planning to do tomorrow, if anything?"

"Boy," Longarm said, scratching his stomach. "You're as cross as an old snapping turtle tonight. If I had some whiskey, I'd wrestle you to the floor and pour some down your gullet."

"If you tried that I'd make sure that you'd be walking around as bowlegged as a barrel hoop tomorrow."

"Whew!" Longarm whistled. "You are really on the prod."

"You bet I am," Carrie said, striding back and forth in front of him. "I've been up here two days and expected that, when you arrived, we'd get together and start getting some answers. But what do I discover? You come here, get

116

a great room, take a nap and then go to the Silver Slipper to play 'rub her bottom' with a woman of ill repute. Then you go upstairs to her room . . . with the entire saloon watching and laughing . . . and rut like a pagan!"

Longarm shook his head. "Are you by any chance a Holy Roller? I mean a real fire-and-brimstone kind of woman?"

"I'm a woman who wants to save her father and expected some help from a United States marshal sent all the way from Denver because he was supposed to be something special."

"Well," Longarm said, "I'm *real* sorry to have disappointed you, Miss Lake. Now why don't you tell me what you've found out about the missing marshals while you've been in this town?"

"I haven't found out anything."

"What?" Longarm raised his eyebrows in question. "Not one thing?"

"Men only want to talk me into going to bed with them. When I start trying to talk about my father and the other missing marshals, they either walk away or demand to know what business it is of mine. And, of course, I can't tell them why I'm up here and that I was hoping that I could work with you to solve the disappearances."

"So you're stuck," Longarm said.

"That's right. You see, a man can come to town and pose as an investor or whatever, but a woman who comes along gets pegged as . . ." She couldn't finish.

"As what?"

"You know! Either a whore or a dishonest woman looking for a way to make money."

"You could play either role very well," Longarm told her. "You've a sharp enough tongue for it."

"Dammit, Marshal!" she cried, whirling and lunging for the door.

Longarm tried to catch her but he tripped on his nightshirt and went sprawling on the floor. By the time he righted himself, Carrie Lake was gone.

It took Longarm quite a while to calm down enough to fall back asleep. He was a man who could put his own mind to rest about most things, but his brief, acrimonious meeting with Carrie had been unsettling. The truth was that he hadn't wanted to work with an inexperienced, hot-headed young woman. Carrie and her temper could get a man killed, and Longarm was sorry that she hadn't stayed in Reno. Better yet, he wished she'd remained in San Francisco. A sharp-tongued woman like that was bound to get him killed.

In fact, Carrie might already have tipped his hand.

Longarm fell asleep just before dawn and didn't wake up until ten o'clock that morning when Herbert lightly tapped on his door.

"I thought you might be ill or something," the proprietor said. "I'm sorry to have awakened you."

"It's time I got up and about anyway," Longarm told the man.

"Mr. Hammond was inquiring about you this morning over breakfast. He said that, if you have some time, he would like to speak to you privately."

"Sure," Longarm said. "Will he be here this evening?"

"I have no idea."

"I'll find him and talk to him," Longarm said. "He seems like he might also be of some value in helping me find a good mine to invest in."

"Oh," Herbert said, "I very much doubt that."

"Why not?"

"Because he's a banker and not a mining engineer."

"I see."

Longarm declined a late breakfast and met Herbert in the parlor a half hour later. "I'm ready to go if you are? Very kind of you to offer to show me around."

"My pleasure."

Cecelia Gordon appeared. "Good morning, Mr. Long. Goodness, you sure slept late and well."

"Yes, I did."

"You must have had quite the time last night. I even thought I heard a woman's voice downstairs in your room in the wee hours of the morning."

"How about that," he said, turning away quickly and heading out the door after the woman's husband.

Longarm spent a pleasant enough afternoon following Herbert Gordon around the Comstock Lode, which was literally honeycombed with underground mines.

"Mr. Long," Herbert said as they stood near an abandoned mine called the Four Aces, "there are so many underground tunnels at all depths that, if they were somehow to be connected in a single line, they would stretch all the way into the Pacific Ocean."

"Are you serious?"

"Most certainly," Herbert told him. "We are standing over a maze of mine tunnels. At first, they collapsed so frequently that men were dying every day. But then a brilliant German engineer named Philip Deidesheimer was brought in by the big mines as a consultant and he devised a system called 'square setting.'"

"What was that?"

"It was a system of short, massive timbers that interlocked, forming large cubes or squares where the miners could work with some degree of safety. These square sets immediately solved the cave-in problem and allowed the miners to go much deeper than ever thought possible. You see, Mr. Long, there were about thirty main ore bodies under our feet. They were irregularly shaped and impossible to locate so the miners had to keep excavating larger spaces. They bored vertical shafts from which they worked outward into hundreds of miles of horizontal tunnels called drifts."

"What was the largest ore body found here on the Comstock Lode?" Longarm asked.

"It was a pocket of pure silver aptly called, the Big Bonanza, and its size is far larger than our Pink Mansion."

"Are you serious?"

"I am," Herbert said. "The Big Bonanza is estimated to have yielded about thirty million dollars worth of ore in 1876."

Longarm whistled with amazement. "And what is the current value being produced?"

Herbert shrugged. "The operating mines still in production aren't about to give those figures up, but you know they wouldn't be in business if they weren't still making a profit."

"That's true. What about these abandoned mines?"

Herbert grinned. "That's the most interesting and exciting part to my way of thinking."

"Why?"

"Because of their untapped potential," Herbert said. "For example, a mine like the one I'm about to show you is a hundred feet deep and has about two miles of horizontal tunnels. The Lucky Lady was a fabulous producer just seven years ago, but then its production began to slip as its costs spiraled. Finally, her owners ran out of money, but I think they were very close to rediscovering a huge pocket of ore."

Even though Longarm wasn't really an investor, he could not help but feel a bit excited. "So what you're saying is that a mine that was abandoned could have been only a few yards from hitting another bonanza?"

"Exactly! Why, if we were blessed with the power to see through rock, we might go down in the Lucky Lady, stand at the face of a wall under the protection of square set timbering and be only inches away from a body of pure gold or silver bigger than . . . than a locomotive!"

"Man," Longarm whispered. "Now wouldn't *that* be something."

"Yes it would, Mr. Long. And it's what drives people like me crazy. I'd be willing to bet everything I own that some of the mines under Virginia City were abandoned within yards, feet or even inches from another stupendous ore body. And, if that discovery was made—and it will be before long—can you imagine the effect it would have?"

"Pretty dramatic, I'd imagine."

"You bet it would be dramatic," Herbert swore. "Suddenly, Virginia City would be famous all over again. Miners would flock from around the world to the new discovery. The town would be rejuvenated. Things would come alive again just like they were back in the sixties and real estate would soon be worth a fortune!"

"Along with your Pink Mansion."

"Of course and so would every other structure now standing. Lumber would be worth dollars a running foot. And it would have to come all the way from California or Lake Tahoe because the eastern slopes of the Sierras were all logged off when Virginia City was booming and the forests haven't really come back yet."

"There would be fortunes to be made at every turn."

"Yes!" Herbert cried. "And don't you want to be a part of it?"

"I sure do," Longarm said, nearly carried away by the fervor in the man's voice.

"Good," Herbert said. "Now let's take a look at the Lucky Lady, which just feels *very* lucky to me."

"Do you own part of it?"

Herbert was reluctant to answer.

"Well," Longarm insisted. "Do you?"

"Cecelia, I mean Mrs. Gordon, and I have invested quite a bit of money in this mine. And I know that it will repay us a thousand fold, if we can just work it a little deeper."

"Can we go down inside the mine today?"

"That's my intention."

"How?" Longarm hoped that this fanatic was not proposing that they descend rickety old ladders or use ropes.

"Relax," Herbert said. "The mine's steam engine is still operable. It will take a few hours before it has enough power, but if you are quite serious about seeing the inside of a Comstock mine I'll be happy to go fire the boiler."

Longarm had never been down in the belly of the Comstock, and he decided to take this opportunity because it might come in handy later on.

"Sure, Herbert. Fire up your boiler and then let's go enjoy something to eat—on me—while we wait for the steam."

"Splendid!" The young man fairly danced as he unlocked and then rushed into a shack where a rusting but still operable steam engine and boiler awaited. "You won't be sorry, Mr. Long. When we get down into this mine you'll see why Cecelia and I are counting on the Lucky Lady to bring us and the entire town fame and fortune."

"I'm sure that I will," Longarm called to the man.

As he waited outside for Herbert to fire up, Longarm smoked a cigar. He liked Herbert but thought this idea of the Comstock Lode being resurrected by a new mining boom was pretty far-fetched.

Up above the town on the flanks of Sun Mountain, he could see hundreds of piles of abandoned tunnels and mine tailings that reminded him of a massive prairie dog colony. How many dreams had come true here and how many, many more had been crushed like the millions of tons of raw ore that was brought to the surface? It would take tough, hard and driven men to live in this barren and inhospitable country. Men who had not long ago fought, whored, gambled and were now interred in the town's many cemeteries.

I hope I don't join them, Longarm thought.

And what if the missing marshals were rotting in some

of the thousands of mine shafts and holes that he could see? How would he ever find them?

Longarm was considering that possibility when a rifle shot echoed over the hillside. He heard the slug whistle past his ear and dove for cover behind some rusting mining machinery.

There was no second shot and no way to pinpoint where the shooter was hidden. Longarm huddled behind his cover. Time passed until Herbert finally appeared from the shack.

"Got things started," he said cheerfully. "Say, Mr. Long, what are you doing lying in the dirt? Are you all right?"

Longarm stood up and brushed himself off figuring the ambusher would have disappeared. He didn't want to tell this man that he was a marshal and that it seemed enemies had already found him. "I'm fine," he lied. "I got careless and slipped then fell."

"You really have to watch your footing around here," Herbert said. "There's so much cable and metal buried that you can easily trip and get hurt. And people have been known to accidentally fall through the ground into a mine shaft and be killed."

"Yeah," Longarm said, eyes scanning the hills, "I can see that this is a very dangerous place."

"It is," Herbert agreed. "But, if you watch your step and don't go wandering off into the brush, you've got nothing to worry about."

Longarm didn't believe it. Not for a single minute.

Chapter 15

Longarm was angry and upset about someone knowing that he was a federal marshal. How did they already know, and what could he do about it except go about his business? And given that his true identity was known to his enemies, was it really worth bothering to pose as a mine investor anymore?

These were his thoughts as they trudged back down to Virginia City for lunch. Herbert Gordon, completely unaware of the attempted ambush, was excited about taking Longarm down into the Lucky Lady Mine and showing him how the Comstock Lode appeared from beneath the earth's surface.

"We're only going down a little more than a hundred feet," Herbert was saying after they ordered lunch and were waiting for their meal in a quiet little café. "But even at that small depth, you'll feel the temperature is warmer. Five degrees or so, I should imagine. And I'll show you where the previous owners hit a modest body of pure silver and how the square setting method has worked so well over the years."

Longarm forced his thoughts back to this man and wondered if he should just confess that he was involved in a charade that no longer had a purpose. "Herbert, how much is this costing you?"

"What do you mean?"

"For the wood to fire the boiler that gives us the steam to go down and then come back up from the bottom of the Lucky Lady?"

"Ahh!" Herbert scoffed. "Don't worry about it. Just the price of some firewood is all."

Longarm nodded, resolving to reimburse the man for both his time and expense. Their lunch soon arrived, and Longarm was pleased to see that it was bean soup and sourdough bread with lots of black coffee and peach pie for dessert.

"Excellent," Longarm said when they finished eating.

"Glad you liked it," Herbert replied. "I think the steam is up and we can go down into the mine now. You'll find it very interesting, Mr. Long. And I hope that you'll also understand why Cecelia and I are so optimistic about getting it back into production. I just know that the Lucky Lady is about to pay off bigger than ever before."

"I hope you're right," Longarm told the man, meaning it. "Let's go have a look."

They were leaving the café when the banker who Longarm had met on the stage coming up from Reno appeared. In fact, Longarm and Hammond nearly collided on the sidewalk.

"Well, what a pleasant surprise!" Hammond said. "I was hoping to see you gentlemen this evening at supper and here we are."

"Good to see you, too," Longarm told the man.

"Yes," Herbert agreed without much enthusiasm. "We were just about to go down into the Lucky Lady for an inspection. Mr. Long is interested in buying a mine or at least some stock, and I think the Lucky Lady would be just his ticket to success."

Hammond raised his eyebrows in question. "I can name other mines that might hold more promise, Mr. Gordon."

"Oh," Herbert said, trying to keep the irritation out of his voice, "I very much doubt that. Well, Mr. Hammond, I expect we'll see you tonight."

The banker drew out his expensive gold pocket watch. "Hold on a minute. I've just canceled a meeting I had this afternoon. Perhaps, if you don't mind, I'll join you at the Lucky Lady."

Gordon wasn't a bit pleased by this news. "Mr. Hammond," he said, "I doubt you'd want to go down there with us. It's dusty and the mine cage that we're going down in is quite small. There's a lot of debris and—"

"Oh nonsense, Herbert. I've got the time and I'd enjoy going down . . . unless you have some reason for me *not* to visit the Lucky Lady." The banker pinned the owner of the Pink Mansion with his eyes. "*Is* there some reason that you don't want me to join you and have a look down there in your mine?"

"Of course not!" Herbert exclaimed much too vigorously. "Why wouldn't I want you to join us?"

"Thank you," the banker said. He turned to Longarm. "I'll only be a minute and then I'll be right with you both. This will be a welcome distraction. I've been sitting too long in meetings and behind my desk. It will be good to go down into the mine and have an adventure."

Longarm didn't know if he much appreciated the term *adventure*, but he kept his mouth shut while Hammond went into the bank to inform his friends of his new plans.

"Dammit, I would far rather Mr. Hammond not go with us," Herbert confessed.

"Why?" Longarm asked. "He might like the looks of it and decide he should invest in your mine."

"I seriously doubt that," Herbert replied, looking upset. "And besides, the man is accustomed to taking over. Cecelia and I don't really want to give up the mine and all the money we've invested."

"Even if the banker offered you a good deal, ensuring a profit?"

"He won't. What the man will do—and I mean no disrespect to Mr. Hammond—but he'll just go down with us and then start acting as if he knows everything about underground mining. He'll criticize the Lucky Lady from top to bottom and have nothing good to say about her."

"And why would he do that?"

"Because it's in his best interest to steer you into other investments! Either that, or try to discourage Cecelia and me to the point where we'd either give up the mine or else sell it for a song."

"I see," Longarm said, not sure that he saw at all. "Well, we don't have to listen to him do we?"

Herbert brightened. "We sure as heck don't."

The banker appeared looking crestfallen. "Gentlemen," he said, "I'm afraid that something has come up and I'll have to pass on our little adventure. I've a sudden complication and need to meet with some people right away. I'm very sorry that I won't be able to inspect the Lucky Lady with you today, but duty calls."

"We understand," Herbert said, not even bothering to look disappointed. "Maybe another time."

"I hope so and I'll see you both for supper tonight at the Pink Mansion."

Longarm shook the banker's hand and then said, "Well, Herbert, I guess it's just the two of us. Let's get started."

"Yes, let's. The steam engine is ready and we ought to be at the bottom in less than thirty minutes."

They hurried up the hill to the mine and Longarm stood back while Herbert operated the steam engine. He watched with fascination and no small amount of apprehension as Herbert raised a metal platform from the bottom of the mine on a thick wire cable that wound around a rusting spool.

"We are going down on that little thing?" Longarm asked, eyeing the swaying platform doubtfully.

"Sure," Herbert said. "The way this is set up I can operate the engine with a switch that moves with the platform. There are four levels leading off into tunnels that were previously worked. We'll pass each one and they're about twenty-five feet apart."

"Does each of these tunnels lead to big open work areas where ore was once mined?"

"Yes," Herbert said. "We can visit them all, if you want, or else go straight down to the bottom."

"Whatever you want," Longarm told the man.

"I think we'll go all the way to the bottom and then stop at each cavern on the way up."

"Just as long as we make it back," Longarm told him.

"Of course we will!" Herbert patted Longarm on the shoulder. "Don't worry because I know what I'm doing. When we're ready to come back to the surface, I flick the switch and the spool reverses to wind up the cable as we're raised to the surface."

Longarm couldn't take his eyes off the tiny platform. "Are you *sure* this thing works?"

"Of course! I used it only three days ago. When I'm not busy trying to fix up the Pink Mansion, I'm over here mining. I've got the lift rigged so that I can raise and lower myself."

"That's a mighty small platform, and it could use a railing."

"Mr. Long, are you afraid of heights?"

"Not at all," Longarm deadpanned. "It's the falling from heights that worries me."

Herbert laughed. "I'll hook you to the cable so you couldn't fall even if you tried. Goodness, Mr. Long. We're only going down a hundred feet! Why, some of the big mines were lowering workers thousands of feet. I promise you this is perfectly safe."

"I sure hope so," Longarm muttered, already beginning to regret the decision to go down.

For just a moment, he almost chickened out and told Herbert Gordon that he wasn't really a mining investor. But something made Longarm bite his tongue and it was probably the idea that he'd miss a better understanding of Comstock mining if he lost his nerve. Also, he might never have another opportunity to go down deep into the belly of Sun Mountain.

"All right," he said, taking a deep breath, "let's do it."

Herbert told Longarm to step over the shaft, which was very narrow and whose bottom could not be seen in the darkness, and then position himself as close as possible to the middle of the swaying platform.

"It will sway violently at first and you might want to jump off, but don't," the man advised. "You'll see that there is a buckle and snap so that you can fasten yourself to the center bar that attaches to the cable. Do that and there is no way you can accidentally fall."

"Okay," Longarm said, swallowing hard as he stepped to the edge of the deep black hole and then forced himself to take a small hop onto the platform, which immediately began to rock crazily back and forth.

Longarm was now standing directly over the hundred foot shaft and gripping the center bar as if it were his life line. "Now what?"

"Take that rope with the snap and fix it to your belt," Herbert told him. "That's the way."

When the man turned to leave, Longarm almost panicked. "Where are you going?"

"Just over here to adjust the valve on the engine so we have the proper steam pressure. Don't worry, we're about ready."

Longarm clung to the center bar and waited, feeling almost seasick as the platform rocked back and forth over the yawning black abyss. Had the steam engine coughed? Oh, hell, if it quit on them halfway down the shaft . . . Longarm couldn't bear to think about that.

Herbert stepped lightly onto the platform, all smiles. He looked like a kid about to enter a candy shop. "Here we go," he said, grabbing a dangling electrical cord attached to a simple on or off switch. "Next stop, the bottom of the Lucky Lady Mine!"

Longarm felt his belly and balls drop to his boots as Herbert snapped the switch and sent the platform hurtling downward in the darkness. He grabbed the center bar with both hands and clung to it with all his might feeling as if he were going to lose his lunch.

Suddenly, the engine high overhead began to whine and the cable shuddered and shrieked.

"What's wrong!" Longarm shouted into the absolute darkness as the cage slammed into the side of the shaft and then seemed to spring upward toward the round hole of blue sky far, far overhead. "Herbert, dammit, answer me!"

But Herbert couldn't answer because he was no longer on the platform. Longarm knew that when he heard the man's dying scream.

Longarm's heart nearly stopped as abruptly as Herbert Gordon's scream did when the man's body struck the bottom of the shaft. Then, there was absolute silence except for the sound of the little platform that Longarm was standing on made striking the sides of the tunnel.

"Herbert!" Longarm yelled.

The silence deepened and that was when Longarm realized that the steam engine up above had also gone dead.

Chapter 16

Longarm's hands were shaking as he rechecked his safety snap. He eased his feet a little farther apart attempting to balance and then steady the swaying platform. "Herbert?"

No answer.

"Herbert, can you hear me?"

Longarm craned his neck back and gazed up at the small circle of sky. The point of light seemed as far as a distant star but he knew that it was only fifty or sixty feet above where he now was suspended.

What the hell had gone wrong? It was obvious that Herbert Gordon had not bothered to fasten himself to the center bar, and that had been the cause of his death drop. *But why wasn't the steam engine huff-huffing up above? Why had everything gone deadly silent?*

Longarm was not mechanically minded but it seemed obvious that a brake had been thrown up above so that cable that held this miserable little platform had been brought to a sudden and violent halt. So violent that it had even shot upward several feet before crashing down to the end of the cable and then slamming off the sides of this narrow shaft.

Mechanical problem? Or an assassin up above?

Longarm knew it had to be one or the other, and since Herbert had used this machinery to lower and then raise himself to the surface many times, Longarm's guess was that an unseen enemy from up above had thrown the brake.

"Hey!" he yelled. "I need help down here!"

"Help?" a voice responded. "I'll give you help all right. Don't move."

Relief flooded through Longarm. "Thanks!" He breathed.

There were a few moments of total silence and then to Longarm's horror a big rock came flying down the shaft. It struck the side of the shaft and began to ricochet back and forth until it hit the platform. The rock crashed to the bottom of the mine. Longarm felt a spray of dirt and small pebbles strike his hat followed by an ominous silence.

"No!" Longarm yelled. "Damn you!"

"Hold on!" the faceless killer above called down to him. "I'm going to send you down some more help!"

"Who are you? Why are you doing this?"

His answer was cruel laughter.

A moment passed and then Longarm saw the flash of an arm and then another rock come barreling down the shaft straight for his head. He threw his weight hard to one side and the rock smashed into the edge of the platform just missing his left foot. The missile struck the bottom of the mine with a dull thud and Longarm knew it had landed on Herbert's broken body.

Longarm drew his sixgun and aimed toward the hole of blue sky. His heart was racing and the platform swaying, but he knew he could not afford to just stand still and wait until whoever it was up above actually hit him with a heavy rock. A rock that would crush his skull, or break his shoulder or arms. No matter what part of his body was hit, Longarm knew that more rocks would come raining down until he was nothing but a bloody pulp.

This time when the shadow appeared high up above followed by an arm and a rock, Longarm fired. And missed.

The rock smashed into the platform and shattered into big, sharp pieces. Longarm felt his cheek open, and then warm blood began to flow.

I've got to get out of here! He won't make the mistake of showing any part of himself again. No, he'll stand back a ways from the mine shaft and hurl rocks into it so he can't be a target. And sooner or later one of those rocks will hit me in the head and I'll be finished.

Longarm holstered his gun and found a match in his coat pocket. He *had* to see if he could somehow get off this platform and certain death.

His match flared and he held up it, but saw nothing but a small circle of rock and timbers about four feet in diameter. Desperate and nearly in a panic, he bent, still clutching the center pole and extended the match downward. That's when he saw that the platform was just a yard or so above a side tunnel.

If I could just get into the tunnel then that rock-throwin' sonofabitch up above couldn't hit me!

Longarm hated like hell to do it, but he blew out the match then unsnapped his safety line. His only hope was to ease over the edge of the platform and then to dangle above the lower part of the mine shaft and try to swing his body into the side tunnel. But the idea was almost insane. Even if he did manage to swing the cage back and forth and get out of this narrow shaft, what then?

Another rock was thrown and began to bounce off the shaft's walls, shattering into fragments that struck Longarm like spears. He had no choice left so he knelt and then slipped over the edge of the platform so that his body was at least partially protected. The location of the side tunnel was fixed in his mind as he began to swing the platform back and forth. When his boots stopped striking the sides and he was sure he was lined up with the side tunnel, Longarm gave a mighty heave and released his grip.

For a split second, he teetered on the lip of the side tunnel and probably would have tumbled backward to his death if the wildly swinging platform itself had not struck him in the back and propelled him into the side tunnel.

A huge rock struck the now empty platform and Longarm gave a cry of rage and fear as he lay in deep powder and tried to slow his heartbeat.

Minutes passed and then a voice called, "Hey, lawman. How's the air down there!"

Longarm tried to still his breathing and not make a sound.

"Hey!" the voice cried again. "Can either you or Gordon hear me? Or are you standing by the Pearly Gates and talking to Old Saint Peter?"

Loud, insane laughter.

Longarm waited and his heart slowed. The man above kept calling down to him, but he finally gave up. A few minutes later, a kerosene lamp was lowered on a rope into the shaft toward where Longarm lay still. No doubt someone peered cautiously over the side of the deep hole looking down to see if Longarm was either dead or clinging to the platform. And equally no doubt the killer above saw the empty platform and logically deduced that another federal lawman had just been eliminated and would never be found.

Longarm heard the soft spray of pebbles cascade down the shaft and then he thought he heard someone walk away from the mine. After that, he didn't hear a thing except the loud thumping of his own desperate heart.

He remained sprawled in the dry powder of the side tunnel for perhaps ten minutes to be absolutely sure that his enemy had gone and left him for dead. It occurred to him that, if the man above even suspected that he was still alive, the sonofabitch might toss sticks of dynamite down the Lucky Lady's shaft hoping to either bury him alive or at least eliminate the cable and small platform.

"Patience," he told himself again and again. "You've survived this much and you'll figure out some way to get back to the surface."

But even as Longarm told himself this, he found it hard to keep up his hopes because the situation was so bleak.

When enough time had passed, he found another match and struck it. Instantly, Longarm saw that he was in a rather large side tunnel supported by big timbers. The tunnel was about eight feet in diameter and he could see that there was a larger cavern or work area only about thirty feet from where he lay. He could also see that there was a set of dusty rails leading from it to the shaft.

Longarm stood up and brushed the dust from his clothes. His hand was smeared with blood, and he gently touched his cheek feeling the ragged wound but knowing it wasn't going to be a problem. Satisfied that no bones were broken and that he had not been seriously injured by the falling rocks, Longarm made his way along the rails to the cavern. His match died and he lit another knowing he had only about five left to give him light or any hope of escape.

He was in what had to be a square set of the kind designed by the brilliant German mining engineer, Philip Deidesheimer. Longarm stood and looked around. He saw broken picks, shovels and a steel ore cart that had long ago been abandoned along with pairs of worn-out leather gloves. There were also a few kerosene lamps but their contents had evaporated so that they were now useless.

Longarm's match died. He then removed his shirt and fumbled in the darkness until he found one of the busted pick handles. He wrapped his shirt around the pick handle and struck another match. As he had hoped, his shirt caught fire and then ignited the dry wood giving him a crude but effective torch.

It took only a few minutes to examine every square foot of the big underground square-timbered cavern. He could see where the early miners had been working gold or silver deposits. But they had been chipped completely out and now there was only the scarred and pocked face of crumbly rock walls.

"What do I do now?" he asked himself.

And even as he asked the question, Longarm knew the simple yet seemingly impossible solution to his problem. He had to get back on top somehow and find out who had killed poor Herbert Gordon and left him for dead.

Longarm walked back into the tunnel until he stood by the shaft. With his flaming torch, he could see both up and down, but the torch's light wasn't strong enough to reach all the way up or down the shaft.

It was clear to Longarm that he was about fifty feet underground. It was equally clear that no one would ever find him here unless it was Cecelia Gordon who would come hunting for her missing husband at suppertime. Or Mr. Hammond the banker who would recall that Longarm and Herbert had been going down into the Lucky Lady Mine.

If they came this evening, Longarm knew that a way would be found to bring him back to the surface. Maybe they could even recover poor Herbert's body at the bottom of this unlucky mine shaft.

But, if neither Mr. Hammond nor Mrs. Gordon showed up at this mine, Longarm knew that he was most likely going to die a lingering, painful death in absolute darkness.

Chapter 17

When Longarm's first torch began to flicker, he fashioned a second torch and continued to wait—and hope—for someone to arrive at the top of the mine shaft and rescue him. But the long, silent hours passed on and on and Longarm consulted his pocket watch again and again throughout the day and then the night that followed.

"They aren't coming for me," he said when his watch told him that he had been trapped in the mine for more than twenty-four hours.

Longarm was aware that he would die of thirst before starvation and that he had about three days before he would weaken to the point where he wouldn't be able to do much physically.

"If I'm to escape this death trap, it will be up to me alone," he told himself. "I've only two more pick handles and then I'll be out of materials for more torches."

Indeed, Longarm had used a number of the worn-out and discarded work gloves to help keep the torches burning. He stood at the edge of the shaft and studied the broken mining platform that dangled, knowing that he would have to get back on it and then try to climb up the braided wire cable.

There was simply no other means of escape.

Longarm found one of the last and best pair of discarded leather work gloves. He put them on and they were as dry as tinder.

Too dry.

He removed the leather gloves and studied the platform and the wire cable. He was strong, and when he was a boy, he'd climbed ropes up into trees by wrapping his legs around the rope and pulling himself upward with the powerful muscles of his arms. Climbing a twisted wire mine cable shouldn't be too much different. And, if he slipped on the cable, the worst that would happen would be that he would come sliding back down to the platform.

It was worth a try. Hell, it was the *only* thing he could try. If he waited another day he would be weak from lack of water.

Because Longarm hadn't drunk anything in more than twenty-four hours, he was dehydrating, but he thought he could summon up enough piss to wet the palms of the leather gloves and give himself a better grip on the cable. So that's what he did. Straining, he pissed a weak stream on both gloves while holding his torch. Then, he put the gloves on, stepped up to the edge of the tunnel and took a very deep breath.

"Do it," he urged himself, gauging how far he'd have to leap to reach the platform.

With great reluctance, Longarm dropped his crude torch and watched it fall into the abyss. When the torch struck the bottom of the shaft he could see Herbert's lifeless body for a few seconds before the torch died and the lower shaft was plunged into absolute darkness.

The only light remaining was that little circle at the top of the shaft. Taking one more deep breath, Longarm jumped out into the darkness and struck the platform. His gloved hands closed in a viselike grip and he hauled himself onto the swaying platform then groped and found the cable. Longarm held it tight for it was his lifeline back to the surface of the earth and his only chance for escape.

"All right, here we go," he said, as he drew himself upward, wrapping his legs around the swaying wire, which was about as thick as the body of a big diamondback rattlesnake.

The stench of his own urine was strong in his nostrils as Longarm began the slow, difficult and dangerous challenge of ascending fifty feet of rusty, and in some cases, badly frayed mine cable. He was grateful for the gloves but wished they weren't so badly used. Again and again as he crawled upward he could feel his hands being torn as the cable wires penetrated holes in the old leather gloves. But at least the gloves did not shred like dried parchment as he'd initially feared.

Longarm lost track of time. As he climbed, he often had to rest and did so by locking his legs tightly around the cable and hanging on for dear life. In the span of fifty feet, he must have craned his neck and gazed upward five thousand times, and at first, he did not think he was making progress. But gradually, far too gradually, he saw the circle of light grow.

Hands torn and bleeding, he finally hauled himself out of the shaft and managed to reach the loading platform where he lay gasping and staring up into the fading light of day. There was no one in sight, and he could see that the sun was almost gone. There were some pink clouds in the sky that looked absolutely beautiful in the final minutes of the day.

I've made it out alive, he thought. *I did it!*

Longarm was so spent and physically exhausted that he could barely think of what to do next. He lay on the old wooden hoisting platform and tried very hard to gather his wits. To give himself some reassurance, he made sure that his six-gun was still in its holster, and he reloaded it with fingers slick with blood.

It was then that Longarm noticed the duff from a smoking pipe. Whoever had sentenced him and poor Gordon to die in the abandoned Lucky Lady mine had been a pipe smoker. Longarm pinched the pipe duff between his thumb and forefinger and inhaled. The pipe tobacco used by the killer smelled rich and aromatic. It was not a blend that would be used by a poor workingman.

Longarm inserted the pinch of unburned duff into his shirt pocket. He would keep it and perhaps it would help him identify the man who had tried to kill him.

Standing took some time and effort. Longarm swayed against the mine scaffolding and gazed down on the Comstock Lode. He then turned his attention to the footprints in the surrounding dust. Longarm recognized his own prints and he thought he could identify those of Herbert Gordon. The third set of tracks would be those of the man who had attempted to bury him in the depths of the abandoned Lucky Lady.

Longarm knelt and measured the length of that third set of tracks. He noted that they were a little shorter but definitely wider than his own footprints, and the leather soles were so new that he could identify stitched seams. Another clue to help him find the man who had so cruelly left him to die, probably never to be found or identified.

Longarm was weaker than he'd thought he would be as he staggered along the worn path toward Virginia City.

He would return to the Pink Mansion and rest the night, and then he would do his level best to find out who had tried to murder him after taking the life of Herbert Gordon. Which reminded Longarm that he would have to tell Mrs. Cecelia Gordon the tragic circumstances surrounding her husband's death. And that, he realized, would be his first unpleasant task.

Puffing and panting, he was forced to climb a small ridge and when he did, Longarm's jaw dropped almost to his knees.

The Pink Mansion was gone, and in its place remained smoking ruins. He could see tendrils of smoke rising into the gathering darkness, and in some places, flames and glowing orange coals.

Longarm blinked, hardly able to believe his eyes. He forced himself to hurry but stumbled so badly he had to revert back to walking because of his weakness and the rough, uneven footing.

When he neared the rubble of the Pink Mansion, he saw a number of people standing around gazing at the charred devastation.

"What happened?" Longarm asked.

A woman turned and her hand jumped to her mouth in shock. "Who are you?"

"I was staying there," Longarm replied, realizing he must look as though he'd emerged from a crypt given the gash on his face, his filthy clothing and his bloodied hands. "How did the fire start?"

"No one knows," a man standing beside the shocked woman said. "It broke out last night. By the time our volunteer fire department could get hoses on it, the flames were a hundred feet high and licking at the moon. There was no way our boys could beat down that inferno. It had its way with the mansion. Burned all night and all of today. I expect it will continue to burn and smoke for another day and night before the ashes go cold."

"What about the Gordons?"

"No one has seen either of 'em. Probably died in their bed. Burned to a crisp, I'd guess."

Longarm knew that Herbert Gordon hadn't been incinerated in the inferno but chose not to reveal this information.

"What about Mr. Arnold Hammond?"

"Who?"

"He was a banker from Reno who was staying at the Gordon's mansion," Longarm explained.

"Did you somehow escape the fire?" the woman asked, seeming to snap out of her spell.

"No," he said. "I was trapped down in a mine."

"Well," the woman said, shaking her head, "you look like you fell down the mine shaft and then you must have had all the piss knocked out of you."

Longarm smelled his hands and knew what she meant. He left the couple and moved in closer to the smoking rubble but knew that he wouldn't see any bodies for quite some time until the place cooled down enough so that he could do a thorough search. The mansion had possessed three fireplaces, two built of bricks and mortar and the main one of rock. Amazingly, all three were still standing with smoke trickling out of their stacks.

"Damn shame," someone said. "The Gordons were nice folks."

"Yeah," Longarm agreed.

Longarm trudged back into Virginia City and entered the Silver Slipper Hotel and Saloon looking like he'd climbed out of a funeral pyre.

"Custis!" Izzy cried when she spotted him in her doorway. "You look more dead than alive!"

"Whiskey," Longarm croaked with his mouth as dry as desert sand. "But first water."

"You'll have plenty of both," the saloon owner promised helping Longarm over to a table and easing him into a chair.

"Bartender, a pitcher of water and a bottle of our best whiskey!"

Moments later, Longarm was gulping water. When the pitcher was emptied, he grabbed the neck of the bottle and took a long, satisfying pull.

"Custis, are you going to make it?"

"Sure," he said wearily.

"We thought you'd been burned up in the mansion along with the Gordons and Mr. Hammond."

"No," he said, smelling his own urine and feeling it burn into the palms of his bleeding hands. "Izzy, could we go upstairs to your room? I need a bath and clean clothes."

"Sure," Izzy said, helping him out of his chair and then upstairs.

Thirty minutes later, Longarm was soaking in a hot bath, smoking a cigar and sipping Izzy's best whiskey.

"You've got a nasty cut on your cheek and the palms of your hands are sliced to pieces."

"I know but I'm fine now," he said.

"Want to tell me what happened?"

Without any extra words, Longarm told the woman about going down into the Lucky Lady mine and then having someone on top release the cable brake. "Herbert plunged to his death at the bottom of the shaft, but I got lucky. After a day, I realized that no one was coming to help. I was able to climb the cable and escape."

"But didn't anyone know you were going down in that abandoned mine?"

Longarm thought only a moment before he said, "As a matter of fact, two people knew. Mrs. Cecelia Gordon and Mr. Arnold Hammond."

"But they probably burned to death in the mansion."

Longarm frowned and smoked in reflective silence for a moment. "That could be the case," he said slowly. "But there's another possibility."

"What?"

"How well did you know Mrs. Gordon?"

"I didn't know her at all," Izzy replied. "But, in a town

this small, you can't help but hear gossip about everyone."

"And what was the gossip about Cecelia?"

Izzy took a pull on Longarm's bottle. "The talk—and I never really believed it—was that Mrs. Gordon and Mr. Hammond were having a torrid and secret affair."

"No kidding?"

"It's not a thing I'd kid about. That kind of talk disturbed me."

"Why?"

"Because everyone liked Herbert Gordon. He was earnest and a dreamer but he was a nice person. Sure, he could get on your nerves with all his excited talk about that Lucky Lady mine that we knew would never pay out again but the world needs a few dreamers."

"Did Mr. Hammond always stay at the Pink Mansion?"

"Yes he did. And sometimes, he'd be there in the daytime when Mr. Gordon was off to the mine or someplace else. It didn't look good to people and that's why there was the talk."

Longarm considered this information and said, "Where there is smoke there is often fire, Izzy."

"So you think that . . ."

"I don't know," Longarm interrupted. "But when the ashes of that mansion's inferno cool, I'm going to be there with a shovel and a rake looking for human bones."

Izzy shuddered. "Grisly work, that."

"Maybe. But maybe not."

"Meaning?"

Longarm studied his lacerated palms and wondered if the urine he'd used on them might aid in their healing. He'd heard that it would.

"Custis, would you *please* answer me?"

"Well, Izzy, if the bodies of Mr. Hammond and Mrs. Gordon *are* found in the charred remains of a bedroom, then we know that the lovers died in a fiery embrace. But, if they're *not* found, then something tells me that they are no longer on this Comstock Lode."

"But where would they go? And why?"

"Good question," Longarm said, taking another pull on the whiskey. "And when I know the answer, I'll probably know what happened to a lot of dead and missing San Francisco lawmen."

Chapter 18

The next day Longarm went to a man named Clancy O'Malley who was the chief of Virginia City's Volunteer Fire Department and said, "Chief, I need to know if anyone died in that mansion fire. How soon can we start going through the ashes?"

"Tomorrow morning," the big Irishman replied. "But you don't need to do that. It's *our* job. We figure to find the remains of Mr. and Mrs. Gordon. Maybe someone else like Mr. Hammond, God bless their poor souls."

"You won't find the body of Herbert Gordon in the ashes."

"And how would you be knowin' that?"

"Because he's resting at the bottom of the Lucky Lady mine. He fell to his death there a few days ago."

O'Malley gaped. "Are you sure?"

"Yes."

"Then we've got to get him out!" the Irishman exclaimed. "Give the poor gentleman a decent Christian burial!"

"That's up to you," Longarm said. "Personally, I think that Herbert would as soon be buried in the Lucky Lady. He loved that mine. Maybe all you need to do is pitch a few

149

wheelbarrows full of dirt into the mine and let the man rest in peace."

"You're crazy!" the Irishman protested. "That's not Christian."

Longarm could see that there was no point in arguing with the man, who went rushing off to get some help in order to retrieve poor Herbert's broken body.

Longarm stood with his arms folded across his chest and watched as O'Malley and five members of the fire department finished searching for human remains buried in the ashes and rubble.

"Nothing?" Longarm asked the man.

"Not so much as a single bone," O'Malley said, shaking his head and slapping ashes from his pants and boots. "We gave it a thorough search and no one died in there."

"That's all I needed to know," Longarm said, turning to leave.

"Wait a minute," the Irishman said. "You've been asking a lot of questions of us; now I've got one for you."

Longarm turned to the man. "What is it?"

"Who the hell are you?"

Longarm saw no reason to hide his identity any longer. What would be the point? "I'm a United States deputy marshal," he admitted, showing O'Malley his badge. "I was sent out all the way from Denver to try and discover who was murdering the federal marshals who came from San Francisco."

O'Malley nodded. "And have you figured it out?"

"I think I have."

"Mind tellin' me?"

"I'm afraid that I do, Chief."

"Wait a minute!" O'Malley demanded. "You've got to at least tell me who trapped you and Mr. Gordon down in the shaft of the Lucky Lady mine."

"I don't know for sure."

"But you have a good idea," O'Malley persisted. "Dammit, I can tell by the look on your face you have an idea."

"That's true. I think you have to ask yourself a question, O'Malley."

His square face reddened with anger. "I've a lot of questions, buster!"

The big Irishman was upset, and Longarm guessed the man had reason to be. First, he'd had to retrieve Gordon's body, now this mystery of no bodies in the ashes.

"All right," Longarm conceded. "I have no real proof but I think that Mrs. Gordon and Mr. Hammond are behind the murders."

"What!"

"Why else would they have torched this mansion and disappeared?"

O'Malley didn't have an answer. "What are you going to do now?"

"I'm going to find that pair and get some answers."

O'Malley scowled at the rubble and at his weary volunteers. "Where could that pair have gone?"

Longarm thought about that for several moments and said, "Either to Reno or to Bodie, and I'm thinking Bodie. I'll speak to the stage company and that will tell me which one."

O'Malley shook his head and ran his ash-stained fingers through a head of thick brown hair. "If they're the ones behind all this murderin' then I sure hope you find 'em and that they swing by the neck and enjoy a swift journey to everlasting hell."

Longarm went to the stagecoach line and learned that neither Cecelia nor Hammond had gone down the mountain to Reno. That just left the Virginia & Truckee Railroad or else rented horses.

"No sir," the railroad ticket seller told him. "I knew both

151

Mr. Hammond and Mrs. Gordon and they sure didn't buy a ticket on my railroad down to Carson City. Why, I expected they'd both perished in that terrible mansion fire."

"Nope."

"Then what happened to 'em?" the man asked, looking confused.

"That's what I'm going to find out."

There was only one livery still operating in old Virginia City. It was located on B Street, and when Longarm arrived there he went directly to the owner and inquired about the missing couple.

"Nope, they didn't rent a buggy or horses from me. Now there was one lady who came in here yesterday to buy a fast saddle horse. She was in a big hurry and had no time for haggling. Paid in cash and lit out of Virginia City like her tail was on fire."

"What did she look like?"

The man gave Longarm a good description; one that left no doubt that the woman was none other than Carrie Lake.

"Did she say where she was going or how long she'd be gone?"

"Hmm," the liveryman mused. "As a matter of fact, she did ask me how far a ride it was down to the old mining town of Bodie."

"Damn," Longarm swore. "Getting back to Mr. Hammond and Mrs. Gordon. Is there anyplace else that they could have rented horses or a buggy?"

"Sure," the man said. "In Gold Hill."

"How far is that from here?"

"About a mile."

"That's all?"

"Yep. But I thought that . . ."

"I know," Longarm said. "You thought they died in the mansion fire."

"Well, didn't they?"

"Nope."

152

Longarm didn't waste any more time with questions. He set off on foot for Gold Hill.

Gold Hill was smaller than Virginia City but it was still impressive with all its rotting and collapsed old buildings and abandoned mines, and the Gold Hill Livery was easy enough to find. Longarm had to wake up the owner, who was napping in a pile of fresh straw. "Excuse me. I have a question."

The man was in his seventies, lean, tall and cranky. "And I have a question for you, mister. Why are you wakin' me up like this!"

"Did a man and woman rent saddle horses or perhaps a buggy in the last few days?"

The man climbed out of the straw. "What business is it of yours?"

Longarm showed the irked liveryman his badge. "I have to know."

"Well, as a matter of fact there was a lady and gentleman who rented a buggy and two horses from me a couple days ago."

"Did they say when they were coming back?"

"Yes, they said they'd be back by now. I ain't too damned happy about 'em overstaying their time and I intend to charge 'em plenty extra."

"I doubt they'll be coming back soon," Longarm told the old man. "In fact, I wouldn't count on them *ever* returning."

"What!"

"They're murderers," Longarm said. "And I'm after them."

"You mean they stole my horses and buggy!"

"Afraid so."

"Why, I'll get me my rifle and hunt them down!"

"I have a better idea," Longarm told the irate liveryman. "Lend me a horse and I'll hunt them down and make sure that your saddle horses and buggy are returned."

"How do I know you'll catch 'em and bring back my horses and buggy?"

"Because I'm giving you my word as a federal officer."

The old man's eyes narrowed with suspicion. "There's lots of crooked lawmen."

"Let me put it this way," Longarm told the man. "What choice do you have but to trust me?"

"I could go after them myself!"

Longarm glanced toward a pen of six or seven saddle horses. "And maybe while you were galloping around looking for those two, someone would steal the rest of your horses. And besides, you don't know where they are going and I think that I do."

"Tell me!"

"No," Longarm replied, getting impatient. "What I'll need is your best mount and some provisions."

"And you expect me to provide for you?"

"I'm almost out of money," Longarm confessed. "And everything I brought with me from Denver was lost in a fire. I'm afraid that I'm your only chance of ever getting your property back, mister."

"Tarnation!" the old man thundered. "What if you stole that badge and are tryin' to rob me like that other pair?"

"I'm not," Longarm said. "Is there a telegraph office in Gold Hill?"

"Sure."

"Then we can wire Denver and they'll confirm what I've just told you."

"But you'd expect me to pay for the telegram. Right?"

"Afraid so," Longarm confessed.

"Shit!"

"We're wasting time," Longarm told the old man. "Are you going to help me help you or not?"

The old goat ran across his yard and kicked a rusty tin bucket high into the air. He cursed and hurled a rock at a mongrel that was ambling up the street but missed by several yards. Finally, he returned to Longarm and said, "All right. It appears that I got no damn choice."

"That's the way that I see it," Longarm told him. "And I forgot to tell you that I'll need to borrow a good rifle. The one you were going to take after Cecelia and Mr. Hammond with ought to do just fine."

The liveryman nearly blew a gasket. "And I suppose you expect me to provide the ammunition!"

"It would be greatly appreciated," Longarm told the furious old man who promptly went storming off to assault a harmless flock of unsuspecting chickens.

Chapter 19

Bodie was just over a hundred miles south along a well-used and picturesque road that sometimes followed the Walker River as it rushed through canyons and lush valleys on its way down into California. But Longarm wasn't in any mood to appreciate the country along the eastern slopes of the towering Sierra Nevada Mountains. Instead he was a man on a mission and that was to not only get to the bottom of the murders, but also to save Carrie Lake from becoming yet another victim of the Comstock Lode murderers.

He passed through Carson City stopping only long enough to have a blacksmith tighten a loose shoe that was floppy on his roan's right forefoot.

"Stranger, these shoes are all worn plumb out," the blacksmith said. "I should replace the four."

"I'm a bit short of funds," Longarm told the man. "Just tighten 'em and I'll be on my way."

"It's your horse," the blacksmith told him looking disappointed.

"No," Longarm said, "it isn't."

"Either way, you're taking a chance with those thin shoes."

"Life itself is nothing but chance," Longarm replied.

Late that afternoon and about twenty miles south of Carson City his tall but high-headed red roan threw one of its overused shoes. Longarm was upset for he had neither the time nor the extra money to be spending on more blacksmithing. So he forced the roan to continue along the road until it started to go lame. Nearing sundown and with the rumble of distant thunder in the high mountains, he came upon Topaz Lake, which was situated right on the border between Nevada and California. It was deep and fed mainly by Sierra runoff. Topaz Lake had once been lined with cottonwoods but they had all been logged off for timbering in the local mines. Coming upon a small settlement, Longarm decided he had no choice but to lay over for the night and find another blacksmith.

"How much do you charge to rent one of those little cabins down by the lake?" Longarm asked a huge woman who looked like a muleskinner.

"Three dollars a night. My cabins rent with firewood for the stove, clean sheets on a good mattress and a hot meal in my kitchen."

"That sounds plenty fair but it's a bit more than I can spend."

The woman was dressed in a man's shirt and baggy pants. Her face was lined and leathery and there was little sympathy in her voice when she said, "Mister, if you ain't got the three dollars, you can sleep on the ground and put your horse in our pen where he'll be well fed. Cost you only one dollar and *you* get the scraps from my cookin' instead of my dogs."

Longarm counted his money. Unfortunately, most of his traveling cash had been lost in his room during the fire along with his extra clothes and belongings. Even his razor and extra ammunition had gone up in smoke.

He had just twelve dollars. "I don't suppose there's a telegraph here in Topaz?" he asked, thinking of sending a wire to his boss in Denver urgently requesting more travel money.

"Did you see any telegraph wires?"

"No. What about down in Bodie?"

"Not too likely," the woman said. "I doubt if anyone there can even spell their own names. Furthermore, you'll find that everything for sale in Bodie is higher'n a hog's back. You won't get a room for the night and a good meal for no three dollars, I'll bet."

"My horse is starting to go lame."

"I noticed that as you were riding up here."

"Ma'am, he has to be re-shod."

"That's obvious."

"Is there anyone here that can do it for a *reasonable* price?"

"Depends on what you call reasonable, mister."

"One dollar," Longarm said, feeling he was in no position to bargain. "I would consider that amount to be reasonable."

"That would not be reasonable, it would be plain stupid," the woman told him. "Mister, in case you haven't noticed, horseshoes ain't free. And then there are the nails to buy not to mention the hardship on the shoer's back."

"How much will it cost?" Longarm asked, knowing he had no choice but to pay the price.

"Mister, since you're kinda handsome and more mannerly than most, I'll do it for just three dollars."

"*You're* the blacksmith in Topaz?" he asked, unable to hide his surprise.

The big woman who might have been thirty or fifty gave Longarm a steely glare. "Mister, here in Topaz, I'm everything. I cook all the meals for the cabin renters, clean up their stink and trash when they leave, hunt for meat, and break wild mustangs as well as shoe lame horses like your roan."

"I didn't mean to . . ."

She cut him off and kept going. "I also trap varmints for their skins, and I even make snowshoes to sell in the winter to poor travelin' fools grown desperate when the snow is deep. And I got a little silver mine up in the mountains I work, but mister, don't even think about trying to follow me up to it and steal from my claim."

"I wouldn't do that," Longarm said. "Because I'm sure that, among all your talents, you are an expert shot."

"Best in Topaz. Best for miles around," she assured him. "I can blow a shittin' sparrow out of the sky with a Winchester rifle."

"That is impressive."

"And I can carry a hundred pound sack of salt and beans in each of my hands a mile nearly straight up the mountain without once stoppin' to rest and suck wind."

Longarm saw the muscles that corded the woman's arms and thickened her shoulders and knew she wasn't bragging.

"All right," he said, knowing he had no choice unless he intended to walk to Bodie, "four dollars and I'll sleep on the ground down by the lake tonight. But I'll need to leave early and have the horse shod and ready to go at first light."

"He'll be ready. Readier than you, I'll wager." The woman stuck out her hand. "My name is Nettie."

"Mine is Custis," he said, feeling as if he'd been tromped on by the hard hoof of an ox.

Longarm paid the big, rough woman and went out to put his lame horse in Nettie's pole corral. Tonight he would use his saddle for a pillow and his saddle blankets to cover him for warmth. He glanced up at the sky and saw that there were dark clouds gathering over the Sierras. He just hoped to hell that there wasn't a storm coming in tonight or he'd be one wet and miserable bastard long before morning.

• • •

It began to pour rain not long after dark. Longarm was soaked to the skin in less than three minutes and he ran back up to the main cabin where the big woman who did everything better than a man and could shoot straight enough to kill a sparrow on the wing lived.

After he knocked on her door a few times, Nettie answered with a pistol in her powerful fist. "What you want now, Custis?"

"It's pouring cats and dogs out here. Couldn't I just sleep on your floor by your fire?"

"Cost you two bits."

Longarm bit back a cussword and nodded in agreement. The rain was almost sleet and he was shivering so hard he could hardly speak. Nettie opened her door and pointed to the floor. "You'll dry out by the stove soon enough."

"Thanks."

"Where's your two bits?"

He dug into his soppy wet pants and gave her the money. "You're sort of a hard woman to deal with, Nettie."

"Learned it from a hard life," she told him. "You're either tougher than the next person or you're weaker. If you're weaker, then you'll wind up suckin' hind tit every time. I never got nothin' that I didn't earn. Ain't nothin' in this world for free. You're a grown man and ought to know that full well, Custis."

"I do," Longarm said, hustling over to the stove. "Mind if I throw a little more wood in the stove so I'll dry out quicker?"

"Guess not. Expect you to chop what you add to the fire, though."

"Of course I will. Did you get my roan shod yet?"

"I'll get to it come daylight."

"Good," he said, pitching wood into the stove and then huddling beside it feeling chilled to the bone.

Nettie disappeared and Longarm soon dried out and warmed up enough to stretch out beside the tin barrel stove, which was red now and crackling with heat. He was dog tired and thought this had been a rough day of travel. Longarm drifted off to sleep but was awakened a short time later.

"Nettie? What the hell are you doin'?"

She was in a man's nightshirt and her big, calloused hand was exploring his private parts.

"Nettie?"

"I'm still a woman," she said in a choked voice that held no small amount of bitterness. "I own this place and have some money. I ain't dirty nor lazy and I am a woman of some worth. In short, I ain't a *real* bad find, mister."

Longarm gulped, not sure what to say or do. "I'm sure you're not, Nettie, but . . ."

"I don't much like it myself but there is no sense in denying the truth."

"Which is?"

"Custis, more often than I care to admit, I still suffer a woman's urges in the night."

Her hand tightened on his manhood as if it were trying to throttle her impulses. Longarm squirmed on the floor. "Nettie, listen to me. I . . ."

She flopped down beside him, big but clean. "Nothin' comes for free, Custis. I know that and I know I'm no beauty to the eye. Never was and never will be. But I still suffer a woman's urges, like I said. And I want you to satisfy 'em right now."

"But . . ."

"I won't charge you the dollar. And I'll shoe your roan for fifty cents."

"How about we make it an even swap all around," Longarm heard himself suggest to his own great surprise.

Nettie was silent for a moment, then she throttled his manhood as if she were choking a chicken. "It's a deal."

He paused only a second and then gasped, "Okay, Nettie. I'll do the best I can for you."

"Don't hurry me. I won't be hurried by a man. I mean to have my pleasure before you have yours."

Longarm was going to ask her if she wanted him on the top or the bottom. But Nettie solved the dilemma by climbing onto him, knees hard on the floor. She outweighed Longarm considerably and it took some time for him to catch his breath and get down to taking care of his end of this deal.

"Come on!" she shouted a few minutes later as the tin stove crackled. "Come on big man!"

Her thighs were crushing his ribs. "I'm trying!"

Longarm wrestled Nettie to the floor and then somehow managed to pin her while he got his manhood buried into something that he would never have wanted to explore had he not been in extremely difficult financial circumstances.

"Slow it down, Custis!"

Longarm slowed, but after awhile, they both got faster and faster until they were shouting and wrestling around on the cold cabin floor. One on top, then the other, and once they banged up against the stove and Longarm got his butt a little scorched.

When it was over, Nettie didn't say a word. She just climbed to her feet and waddled silently back into her room.

"Hey!" he yelled when he could catch his breath. "Nettie, I want to know if you think it was a fair trade or not."

He heard the big woman let out a long, satisfied groan and then say in a voice almost girlish, "It was *real* fair, Custis. If you want to stay on permanent, we can work out a deal but I won't abide a lazy man, not even one as good lookin' and as well-hung as yourself."

Despite himself, Longarm chuckled. He sure as hell wouldn't stay here at Topaz Lake, but there was something about Nettie that he liked and admired. Furthermore, he was glad he had lived up to his part of their bargain.

Chapter 20

With fresh shoes on all four of his roan's feet, Longarm rode into the mining town of Bodie with his hat pulled down low and his eyes missing nothing or nobody. He was surprised at how many people were living in this harsh, inhospitable bowl of high desert sagebrush. Longarm guessed that the population here was at least a thousand, and there were plenty of saloons and whorehouses on both sides of the street. He had heard over the years that Bodie was as wild and lawless as any town on the western frontier.

Longarm looked in vain for a marshal's office and settled for a livery where he could put up the roan. It was his intention to begin by searching for Carrie Lake, and he sure hoped she hadn't been killed like her father and the other lawmen.

"Stayin' long, mister?" the liveryman asked.

"Not longer than I have to."

The man chuckled. "Now that is a damned poor attitude, if I ever heard one. Bodie isn't *that* bad."

"From what little I've seen so far, it isn't that good, either. How much would you charge to board my horse for a night?"

"Two dollars a day gets you grass hay. Two dollars and

a dime gets him grain. And since the grass hay ain't too fine, I'd recommend you spend the extra dime."

"You're not only a poet, but a thief," Longarm told the man, paying him for two nights in advance. "Where is a good place to stay and eat?"

The liveryman gave him some suggestions and then went about his business, leaving Longarm to consider his first move. What he needed to do, he had already decided, was to somehow find Carrie Lake and then Arnold Hammond and Cecelia Gordon. After that, he didn't know exactly what might happen. He did need some proof, not only of the killings of the San Francisco lawmen but also that it had been Hammond the supposed banker who had tried to bury him in the Lucky Lady mine.

Longarm still had the duff of pipe tobacco in his shirt pocket but it had lost most of its rich aroma.

"Well," he said to himself, "I just hope I see them before they see me."

He walked up the main street and decided that half the men in Bodie were either drunk or on their way to being drunk. Prostitutes were thicker than fleas on a hound dog, but he also saw that there was a lot of money being spent by the hordes of miners. That meant that the mines around this town, in contrast to those up in Virginia City, were booming.

Longarm saw a place called Bodie Café and realized he was famished. He stepped up to the window where the owner had posted a menu and saw that he could get a cup of coffee, a bowl of chili and all the sourdough bread he wanted for seventy-five cents. That was probably a bargain for this town so he went inside and found a little table where he could sit with his back to the wall.

Carrie Lake appeared out of the kitchen wearing an apron and carrying a coffeepot. Longarm watched her pour several cups of coffee for the other patrons and then she turned and saw him seated.

The coffeepot slipped from her hand and coffee splattered all over the wooden floor and on everyone's lower pant legs. One well-dressed man that Longarm judged to be a professional gambler took offense as he stared at his pants.

"Dammit!" he swore. "These trousers were clean and now you've stained them because of your clumsiness."

"Sorry."

"That isn't good enough! You'll pay to have my trousers cleaned and pressed."

Apparently, Miss Carrie Lake was not the kind of young woman who responded well to rudeness. "Mister," she snapped, "I said I was sorry and that's all that you're going to get."

"Why you . . ."

The gambler didn't have time to finish whatever insult he was intent on hurling at Carrie because Longarm stood up and shoved him over backward in his chair. He landed on his back in the steaming pool of spilled coffee.

Longarm watched the gambler make a grab for his hidden derringer. With a quick kick of his boot he caught the man in the forearm hard enough to send the little gun flying.

"Mister," he said, "your bad manners are exceeded only by your stupidity. Now get out of here before I do you serious harm."

The gambler was a good-sized man and younger than Longarm but he wisely decided he was not up to a fight with the towering figure standing above him. Without another word, he scrambled to his feet and hurried outside, slamming the door in his wake.

Longarm returned to his chair. "I'll have the chili and sourdough," he told Carrie. "Heavy on the sourdough and butter."

"What about the coffee?"

"Any left?" he asked with an easy smile.

"I think the cook can brew another pot . . . after we

wash this one. How are you, Custis W. Longfellow? Are you still looking at mining investments?"

"I am," he said, relieved that she remembered his alias.

"And how is your health these days? Not swimming in cold rivers anymore, are you?"'

"Not if I can help it," he said, recalling how she'd helped drag him out of the Truckee River. "And you?"

"I'm getting by, Mr. Longfellow. We really need to talk."

"The sooner the better," he agreed.

She leaned closer so that her next words wouldn't be overheard. "I'll take a break after you finish eating. Meet me in the alley behind this café."

"Might take awhile," he warned. "I'm hungry."

"And you smell like a goat. What happened to your cheek and hands?"

"Long story," he told her. "And not a very happy one."

"I'll get you served and fed," Carrie told him as she cleaned up the spillage.

An hour later, Longarm was standing in the alley when Carrie appeared, still wearing her apron. Her raven-black hair was pulled back in a bun, and she looked tired and overworked but her green eyes were still bright with intensity and intelligence.

"What are you doing here?" she asked without preamble.

"Looking for you among others. Have you found out anything about your father?"

Her eyes clouded with sadness. "No. I'm slowly coming to accept the fact that my father is dead along with the other lawmen from San Francisco."

Longarm nodded with sympathy and understanding. "That's likely the sad truth," he told her. "And what we have to do now is find out who killed them."

"That's the only reason I'm in Bodie," Carrie said.

Quickly, Longarm told her about the banker he'd met

named Arnold Hammond and also about Mrs. Cecelia Gordon. He ended up by saying, "They might very well have changed their names. But I think they've come here and that they might be posing as husband and wife."

"That's *exactly* what they are doing," Cecelia said with excitement. "I knew they were up to something the moment they arrived. Remember that I spent more time in Virginia City than you did, and they were both rather prominent on the Comstock Lode. Mrs. Gordon always seemed to act superior but what happened to Herbert Gordon? He was such a sweet man."

"He fell to his death in the Lucky Lady mine and I almost joined him. Does Mr. Hammond ever smoke a pipe?"

She thought a moment. "I believe he does. I can't be sure, though. Do you think that he and Mrs. Gordon have something to do with the murders?"

"I'm almost certain of it."

Longarm told her about the fire that had completely consumed the Pink Mansion and how he had found tobacco duff from a pipe up on the hoisting platform of the Lucky Lady.

"Then arrest them at once!" she urged.

"I can't do that without proof."

"But how . . ."

"I don't know," he interrupted. "What I do know is that they probably think I am rotting at the bottom of the mine shaft. Furthermore, I expect that, if they saw me here, they would try to have me killed and most certainly would not answer any questions."

"And you think Mrs. Gordon had her poor husband killed?"

"Yes. She and Mr. Hammond are obviously lovers and in league for the money."

"What can I do to help you bring them to justice?"

Longarm thought a moment. "I need a room and a disguise. And I need funds. I'm almost broke because my travel money went up in flames. Can you help me?"

"I'll do whatever it takes," she promised.

"Good! Then let's find me a room and a disguise. I need to be able to move around and start watching that pair. They are not the kind to hang around for long in a miserable town like this. If Hammond and Cecelia Gordon have accomplices, we'll identify them and make our move in a hurry."

Carrie dug into her dress pocket and gave Longarm ten dollars. "It's all I have right now but I'll get you more later."

"Where can I stay? It should be a place where we can meet without causing a lot of talk."

"I'm staying at the Harper House. It's supposed to be for women only but I'm sure the landlady who owns it would take you in if you showed her your badge and swore her to secrecy."

"All right."

Longarm got directions to the Harper House and just before leaving, he warned, "If this woman at the hotel should have a loose tongue and let it be known that I'm a federal marshal, both our lives will be in grave danger. Are you sure she can be trusted?"

"Yes. Her name is Mrs. Ida Wilson. Speak to her in private and tell her that you're not only a lawman, but my fiancé."

"Why the second part?"

"Because," Carrie said, "Mrs. Wilson is a romantic."

"In that case, why don't we share your room and save the money?"

"Because," Carrie said, "I'm neither a romantic . . . nor a fool."

"Meaning?"

"Meaning I don't think you can be trusted in compromising circumstances."

"I hope to prove you wrong on that," Longarm said with a wink. "And how about finding me a disguise?"

"What did you have in mind?"

Longarm thought about that a moment. "I think a derby to replace my Stetson and a pair of weak eyeglasses might do."

"I can't imagine you with a derby and spectacles."

"I'm hoping that Cecelia and Hammond can't either," he said. "And I suppose I could cut off my handlebar mustache."

"Don't," she told him. "For that would be a real travesty."

Longarm smiled and rolled the tips of his handsome mustache. "Yes," he said. "I suppose it would be. Too bad that I don't have time to grow a full beard."

She touched his cheek. "That would be another travesty, Custis. Just stick with the spectacles and the derby hat. And perhaps I can find another coat for you to wear."

He told her his coat size as she went back into the café using the rear entrance. *Smart girl*, he thought. *And still lovely despite all the tragedy and strain she is facing here in wicked, wicked Bodie.*

Chapter 21

"Well," Ida Wilson said, looking suspiciously at Longarm, "I ain't too sure about letting you stay here so close to my girls. I don't take in male boarders because they're all dirty and troublesome."

"I'd be grateful if you made an exception for me," Longarm said, retrieving his badge. "And after all, I am a United States marshal."

"That's the only reason I'm even considering your request."

"But, Mrs. Wilson, you can't tell *anyone* that I'm a lawman."

"Of course I can't!" Ida snapped. "This town is filled with outlaws and you wouldn't last a day if they knew you carried a hidden badge."

"Thanks," Longarm said to the smallish and proper landlady. "I'm trusting you with my life by revealing my true identity to you."

"Don't worry," she told him. "I'm not one to gossip and plenty of that goes on here in Bodie that should never be told."

Longarm nodded with understanding. Ida Wilson was a woman in her late sixties and he supposed she was a fairly recent widow because there were pictures of her late husband everywhere. He looked like a stalwart fellow, round-faced with a big walrus mustache and great mutton-chop whiskers.

"I'll be needing a bath as soon as you can get around to it," he told her.

Ida wrinkled her nose. "Your bath will be ready in about an hour. What about your clothes?"

"What about them?"

"Well," Ida said, "they're filthy. Would you like your suit cleaned and pressed? I got a Chinaman that will launder your dirties and fix you up to look respectable. I can't imagine that Miss Lake would want to be seen with anyone so scruffy. And what about that wound on your cheek?"

"It will heal soon enough," he told the woman.

"Mr. Longfellow, you look like you've been through hell and back," she said. "Get out of that suit and underwear and leave them outside your door for the Chinaman."

"Thank you, Mrs. Wilson."

"You're welcome. Don't get killed in Bodie. Miss Lake has had enough sorrow without you adding to it, and I doubt the poor girl has enough money to give you a decent burial."

"Yes, ma'am."

Later that afternoon when Carrie arrived she brought Longarm a black derby and worn waistcoat along with a pair of thick spectacles. Longarm tried the hat and coat on and found them a good fit, but the spectacles were a disaster.

"Carrie, I can't even see the hand in front of my face!" he complained, waving his hand back and forth before his blinded eyes. "I'd be running into posts and everything else, if I wore these twin telescopes."

"Well," she said, sounding a little peeved, "I can't help that. Why don't you wear them far down on your nose so that you can peer over their tops?"

He tried that but they kept slipping over the end of his nose. "I'll just have to do with the black derby and this flea bitten coat. "What did you do, pick it off some drunk who passed out on the street?"

"You guessed it, Custis. But at least I can see that you've bathed and shaved. A definite improvement."

"Thanks. Let's go find Hammond and Gordon."

"Yes," she said, "let's."

The business district of Bodie wasn't that big, and it wasn't long before they spotted the couple exiting a local bank with a well-dressed but portly man in tow. Arnold Hammond slapped the fat gentleman jovially on the back and Cecelia Gordon gave him a dazzling smile. The three were talking rapidly and they climbed into a buggy, probably the one that they'd stolen from Gold Hill.

"What do you think they are up to now?" Carrie asked as they observed from their hiding place.

Longarm watched them drive out of Bodie and then turn east into the foothills where very little mining activity was taking place. "If I had to guess, I'd say that the fat fella was being set up like a pigeon about to be plucked."

"You mean that they're going to kill him?"

"Yes, but they'll rob him first," Longarm answered.

"So what do we do now?"

Longarm was already asking himself the same question. If he was correct, the fat man might be on his way to a mine shaft from which he'd never return.

"We'd better follow them," Longarm decided. "Carrie, do you have a gun or rifle?"

"I have both but they're in my room at the Harper House."

Longarm was wearing his six-gun and derringer. "My rifle is there, too. Where is your horse?"

"At the Acme Livery just up the street."

That was where his roan was boarded. "All right," Longarm told her, "let's go!"

It took them longer than expected to meet back up and then get their horses saddled. Longarm checked out Carrie's rifle and it passed his inspection. He also made sure they each had big canteens filled with fresh water before they headed off into the high desert. By then he was really getting worried about the unsuspecting investor who might well be taking his last buggy ride.

"Come on!" Longarm shouted, whipping the roan into a fast gallop as his derby flew off into the air. Longarm was in too much of a hurry to stop and retrieve the hat because there was absolutely no time to waste if the fat man's life was about to end.

They circled town and accidentally crossed several mining claims in their urgent need for haste. Longarm realized this when miners came running out of their mines or rock hovels waving guns and cussing.

"There are the buggy's tracks!" he said, forcing the roan toward a rutted road that tracked up into the foothills and then disappeared over a ridge. "Come on, Carrie!"

She was mounted on a sorrel mare that was not built for speed. It was a short-legged little mare, good-looking but old and gentle. Still, Carrie was doing her best to force the mare to try and keep up with Longarm's roan.

He drew rein at the top of the ridge and shielded his eyes to stare into the vast sea of sagebrush and broken rock.

"Do you see them!" Carrie shouted when she finally caught up.

"I think so." Longarm pointed. "That black spot on the far horizon just going over that ridge. See it?"

"That's them all right. Come on!"

Carrie sent her mare down the road at a gallop, but the

poor thing was already winded. Longarm wondered how far or fast he could go before the mare quit or died.

They galloped another two miles, and when it became obvious that the sorrel was about to drop, Longarm pulled up on his reins and said, "Tie the mare up to that sage bush and climb on the back of this roan. There's no sense in killing a decent and willing horse."

"Not even to save the life of a human?"

"I doubt that they're taking the heavy man too many miles from Bodie," Longarm replied. "They only have to go far enough to be out of sight of any witnesses."

Carrie tied the exhausted sorrel and managed to climb up behind Longarm. Moments later, they were galloping toward the second ridge where they'd seen the buggy vanish.

When they reached the ridge, Longarm reined the laboring roan up short and dismounted. "There," he said, pointing toward the buggy, which was empty and resting in a small canyon with a mine tunnel and a big pile of rock tailings. "That's where they've gone."

"Why are we stopping now? Let's just ride there as fast as we can and stop them before they murder the poor man."

"I'd do that," Longarm said, "except that there's a good chance they're not working alone. They've killed too many experienced lawmen probably both here and on the Comstock Lode. I'm pretty sure that they'll have a friend or two waiting in that mine tunnel ready to do the dirty work."

"But we can't just sit here and wait!"

"No," Longarm agreed, "we can't. You ever meet an Apache?"

"No. Why do you ask?"

"Because they are the best at sneaking up on something in broken country like this, and we're going to have to try and do the same." He glanced off to his right. "There's a

177

dry arroyo that passes only about a hundred yards to the east of that buggy. We'll use it for cover then take it from there."

"I hope you know what you're doing, Custis."

"It's never the same," he told her. "My guess is that there are at least one, but more likely two, men waiting in that mine for Hammond and the widow Gordon."

"You take them, and I'll take responsibility for Cecelia and Arnold."

"It's a deal," Longarm said. "But don't underestimate that pair. They've got a lot to answer for and a lot to lose."

"I know, starting with my father."

Longarm led the way to the arroyo, and they moved as fast as possible along it until they came as near as they could to the empty buggy. There was still no one in sight, but they could see the mine shaft clearly now.

"What next?" Carrie asked, clutching her rifle.

"Cover me," he said. "I'm going in."

"Alone?"

"It's the best way. I'll try to catch them all by surprise and get their hands in the air, but if something goes wrong, I'll come out flying. Can you hit anything with that rifle?"

"I'm a poor shot," she admitted. "But I might get lucky."

"Just don't accidentally shoot me," he warned a moment before he pulled Carrie to his chest and kissed her on the lips.

"What was that for!" she protested, reeling back and flashing those angry green eyes.

"Just in case I don't get a second chance I don't want to leave this world with any regrets."

The anger left her eyes and she smiled. "If we come out of this all right I'm going to make sure you get *more* than a kiss, Custis W. Longfellow."

"Promise?"

"I promise," she told him. "Just don't get killed in that mine."

178

"I'll do my best."

Longarm jumped out of the arroyo and sprinted to the buggy. He'd decided to leave his rifle with Carrie and rely on his six-gun and the derringer he carried attached to his watch chain because it was likely to be close, deadly work in the mine tunnel.

Chapter 22

After his near fatal experience in the Lucky Lady mine, the last thing that Longarm wanted to do was to enter another dark and deadly hole in the ground. But there was no choice so he went into the tunnel stepping light on his feet and with his revolver up and cocked. He paused for a few minutes to let his eyes adjust to the darkness and then crept forward hearing the faint whisper of voices. It was then that he smelled the familiar aroma of a fine pipe tobacco. The same tobacco he'd found on the Lucky Lady's hoisting works in Virginia City.

Suddenly, the tone of the voices grew louder, shrill and angry. Longarm knew that there was no more time to waste so he hurried forward. The tunnel was about six feet tall so he had to bend forward or strike his head on its uneven ceiling.

A gunshot boomed out of the darkness ahead and Longarm broke into a run. He rounded a corner that he almost missed and there they were, Arnold Hammond, Cecelia Gordon and two gunmen, just as he'd expected. They were gathered in a well-lit cavern about the size of a small horse barn. Longarm could see a heavy wooden box or two, provisions and various mining tools.

The fat man was down but he wasn't quite finished. He had been shot in the head but was still moaning and thrashing wildly about in his final death throes. To add to the mayhem, Cecelia was screaming at one of the gunmen to put the dying man out of his misery.

"Hold it!" Longarm bellowed, just as the gunman was about to administer a final, deadly bullet.

The two gunmen wheeled and fired but Longarm was partially hidden in shadows while they were fully visible. It gave Longarm the advantage and he used it and the sharp corner of the tunnel well to shield most of his body. He placed a bullet in the first gunman's chest knocking him to the rock floor. The second gunman fired wildly and Longarm's slug tore a gaping red hole in his throat.

"Freeze!" Longarm shouted.

Arnold Hammond should have known better than to try to shoot it out, but perhaps the sight of so much death and blood had momentarily deranged his mind. Whatever the reason, the man fumbled for his gun even as Cecelia tried to blow out a kerosene lamp and plunge the cave into total darkness.

Longarm shot Hammond as the light went out and then he fired his last round where last he'd seen the murderess.

He would never know if his bullet hit Cecelia. All he remembered when he roused from unconsciousness was that his head was being cradled in Carrie's lap just like it had been beside the Truckee River when he'd nearly drowned.

"What happened in there?" he asked, dazed and confused.

"There was an explosion. I heard the boom and saw smoke and dust pouring out of the mouth of the mine. I ran in, stumbled over your body, which was lying next to a cave-in, then, somehow dragged you outside."

He blinked up at the warm sun and clear blue sky. "An explosion?"

"Yes. I have no idea what happened in there."

"My last shot," he whispered. "I must have hit that box and it held dynamite inside. Had to be that."

Carrie leaned over and kissed his dusty, torn cheek. "They're all gone. No chance that anyone survived in that mine. I'm so sorry about the heavy man, and we'll never know the others who were murdered. All the investors and lawmen were no doubt murdered and dumped in the thousands of Comstock Lode mine shafts, never to be given proper burials."

"Yes, Arnold Hammond and Cecelia had their hand in killing all of them," Longarm told her, knowing that this girl had to face that reality. "I'm sorry, too, Carrie, especially about your father."

The woman's tears began to fall steadily on Longarm's battered face, and he closed his eyes thinking that they felt very much like a soft, forgiving rain.

Watch for

LONGARM AND THE LOST PATROL

the 315th novel in the exciting LONGARM
series from Jove

Coming in February!

Explore the exciting Old West with one of the men who made it wild!

JAKE LOGAN
TODAY'S HOTTEST ACTION WESTERN!

J. R. ROBERTS

THE GUNSMITH